DEATH of a
✧.✦✧DREAMER✧.✦.✧

DEATH of a DREAMER

A HAMISH MACBETH MYSTERY

M. C. BEATON

WHEELER

CHIVERS

This Large Print edition is published by Wheeler Publishing, Waterville, Maine USA and by BBC Audiobooks Ltd, Bath, England.

Published in 2006 in the U.S. by arrangement with Warner Books, Inc.

Published in 2006 in the U.K. by arrangement with Lowenstein-Yost.

U.S. Hardcover ISBN   1-59722-230-5   (Hardcover)
U.K. Hardcover ISBN 10 1-4056-3739-0   (Chivers Large Print)
U.K. Hardcover ISBN 13 978-1-405-63739-8
U.K. Softcover ISBN 10 1-4056-3740-4   (Camden Large Print)
U.K. Softcover ISBN 13 978-1-405-63740-4

The text of this Large Print edition is unabridged.
Other aspects of the book may vary from the original edition.

Set in 16 pt. Plantin.

Printed in the United States on permanent paper.

British Library Cataloguing-in-Publication Data available

Library of Congress Cataloging-in-Publication Data

Beaton, M. C.
    Death of a dreamer : a Hamish Macbeth mystery / by
    M.C. Beaton.
       p. cm. — (Wheeler Publishing large print hardcover)
    ISBN 1-59722-230-5 (lg. print : hc : alk. paper)
    1. Macbeth, Hamish (Fictitious character) — Fiction.
    2. Police — Scotland — Highlands — Fiction.   3. Women
    — Crimes against — Fiction.   4. Highlands (Scotland) —
    Fiction.   5. Artists — Fiction.   6. Large type books.   I. Title.
    II. Series.
    PR6052.E196D385 2006
       823'.914—dc22   2006002244

To

Alice Boatwright
and
Jim Mullins,

with
affection

CHAPTER ONE

So, if I dream I have you, I have you,
For, all our joys are but fantastical.
                                    — John Donne

It had been a particularly savage winter in the county of Sutherland at the very north of Scotland. Great blizzards had roared in off the Atlantic, burying roads and cottages in deep snowdrifts. Patel's, the local grocery shop in the village of Lochdubh, sold out of nearly everything, and at one point it was necessary for rescue helicopters to drop supplies to the beleaguered inhabitants.

And then, at the end of March, the last of the storms roared away, to be followed by balmy breezes and blue skies. The air was full of the sound of rasping saws and the thump of hammers as the inhabitants of Lochdubh, as if they had awakened from a long sleep, got to work repairing storm damage.

The police station was comparatively

sheltered below the brow of a hill and had escaped the worst of the ravages of winter. Police Constable Hamish Macbeth found that the only thing in need of repair was the roof of the hen house.

Archie Macleod, one of the local fishermen, went to call on Hamish and found the lanky policeman with the flaming red hair up on top of a ladder, busily hammering nails into the roof of the hen house.

"Fine day, Hamish," he called.

Glad of any diversion from work, Hamish climbed down the ladder. "I was just about to put the kettle on, Archie. Fancy a cup of tea?"

"Aye, that would be grand."

Archie followed Hamish into the kitchen and sat at the table while Hamish put an old blackened kettle on the wood-burning stove.

"Got much damage, Archie?"

"Tiles off the roof. But herself is up there doing the repairs."

Hamish's hazel eyes glinted with amusement. "Didn't feel like helping her, did you?"

"Och, no. The womenfolk are best left on their own. How have you been doing?"

"Very quiet. There's one thing about a bad winter," said Hamish over his shoulder as he took a pair of mugs down from a

8

cupboard. "It stops the villains driving up from the south to look for easy pickings in the cottages."

"Aye, and it keeps folks sweet as well. Nothing like the blitz spirit. How did that newcomer survive the winter, or did herself take off for the south?"

The newcomer was Effie Garrard. Hamish had called on her last summer when she first arrived, and had been sure she would not stay long. He put her down as one of those romantic dreamers who sometimes relocate to the Highlands, looking for what they always describe as "the quality of life."

"I sent gamekeeper Henry up to see her last month, and he said the place was all shut up."

The kettle started to boil. As he filled the teapot, Hamish thought uneasily about Effie. He should really have called on her himself. What if the poor woman had been lying there dead inside when Henry called?

"Tell you what, Archie. I'll take a run up there and chust see if the woman's all right." The sudden sibilance of Hamish's highland accent betrayed that he was feeling guilty.

That afternoon, Hamish got into the police Land Rover, fighting off the attempts of his dog, Lugs, and his cat, Sonsie, to get into it as well. "I'll take you two out for a walk later," he called.

He saw the Currie sisters, Nessie and Jessie, standing on the road watching him. The car windows were down, and he clearly heard Nessie say, "That man's gone dotty. Talking to the beasts as if they were the humans."

Hamish flushed angrily as he drove off. His adoption of the cat, a wild cat, had caused a lot of comment in the village, people complaining that it was impossible to domesticate such an animal. But Sonsie appeared to have settled down and had showed no signs of leaving.

Effie Garrard had bought a small one-storey cottage up in the hills above Lochdubh. It had a roof of corrugated iron, stone floors, and a fireplace that smoked. When Hamish had first visited her, he found her to be a small woman in her forties, sturdy, with brown hair speckled with grey, a round red-cheeked face, and a small pursed mouth. She had gushed on about the majesty of the Highlands and how she planned to sell her "art works" in the local shops.

If she were still alive, and he hoped to God she was, he expected to find that she had packed up and gone, all her fantasies of a highland life shattered.

But as he approached her cottage, he saw smoke rising up from the chimney. Maybe she had sold it to someone else, he thought, and because of the rigours of the winter which had kept most people indoors, he hadn't heard about it.

But it was Effie herself who answered the door to him. "You should really get the phone put in," said Hamish. "Something could have happened to you during the winter, and we'd never have known if you needed help."

"I've got a mobile."

"Does it work up here? There still seem to be blank spots all over the Highlands."

"Yes, it works fine. Are you coming in for tea?"

"Thanks." Hamish removed his cap and ducked his head to get through the low doorway.

The living room and kitchen combined had a long work table with a pottery wheel on it. On the table were a few vases and bowls glazed in beautiful colours.

"Yours?" asked Hamish, picking up a little bowl of sapphire blue and turning it around in his fingers.

"Yes. Mr. Patel has taken some, and the

11

gift shop at the Tommel Castle Hotel has taken a good few more. I didn't do any business during the winter because of the bad weather, but I'm hoping for sales when the visitors come back."

There were paintings of birds and flowers hanging on the walls, each one an exquisite little gem. Hamish was beginning to revise his opinion of Effie. She was a talented artist.

"I'm surprised you survived the winter up here," he said.

"I didn't need to. Coffee or tea?"

"Coffee would be grand. Just black. What do you mean, you didn't have to?"

"I went to stay with my sister in Brighton, and so I escaped the worst of it. Do sit down and don't loom over me."

Hamish sat down on a hard chair at a corner of the work table while she prepared coffee. "Odd," he said. "I thought the Highlands would have driven you out by now."

"Why? This is the most beautiful place in the world."

Yes, thought Hamish cynically, if you can afford to get out of the place for the winter.

Aloud, he said, "Oh, I put you down as one of those romantics."

12

"There is nothing up with being romantic. Everyone needs dreams. Here's your coffee."

Hamish looked at the little blue bowl. "That bowl. Is it for sale?"

"Of course."

"How much?"

"Fifty pounds."

"Fifty pounds!" Hamish stared at her.

"It's a work of art," she said calmly. "Fifty pounds is cheap at the price."

A hard businesswoman as well, thought Hamish. Still, it meant he had been wrong about her. Romantically minded newcomers had caused trouble in the past.

In April there was one last blizzard — the lambing blizzard, as the locals called it — and then the fine weather returned, and by June, one long sunny day followed another. Memories of the black winter receded. It stayed light even in the middle of the night. Amazingly, for Hamish, there was still no crime, not even petty theft.

He was strolling along the waterfront one fine morning when he was stopped by a tall man with an easel strapped on his back who said he was looking for accommodation.

"I don't think there's a place here with a studio available," said Hamish.

The man laughed. "I'm a landscape

painter. I work outside." He thrust out a hand. "I'm Jock Fleming."

"Hamish Macbeth. You could try Mrs. Dunne along at Sea View, just along the end there. You can't miss it."

Jock looked down at the dog and the cat, waiting patiently at Hamish's heels. "That's an odd pair of animals you've got there," he said.

"They're company," said Hamish dismissively.

"Really? It's a good thing I'm not superstitious, or I'd be crossing myself," said Jock with an easy laugh. "A wild cat and a dog with blue eyes!"

Hamish grinned. He took an instant liking to the artist. He was a powerful man in, Hamish judged, his early forties with shaggy black hair streaked with grey. He had a comical, battered-looking face and seemed to find himself a bit of a joke.

"When you've got settled in," said Hamish, "drop by the police station and we'll have a dram."

"Great. See you."

Hamish watched him go. "Well, Lugs," he said. "That'll be one incomer who won't be any trouble at all."

Hamish was disappointed as two days

passed and Jock did not call for that drink. But on the third day, as he walked along the waterfront in the morning, he saw Jock at his easel, surrounded by a little group of women.

Walking up to the group, Hamish said, "Move along, ladies. The man can't do any work with you bothering him."

"I don't mind," said Jock cheerfully. "I like the company of beautiful ladies."

Freda, the schoolteacher, giggled and said, "He's giving us lessons. Why don't you run along, Hamish?"

"Yes," agreed Nessie Currie. "Go and catch a criminal or something."

"I'll see you later for that dram, Hamish," called Jock as Hamish walked off.

I hope that one isn't going to turn out to be a heartbreaker, thought Hamish. He decided to visit Angela Brodie, the doctor's wife.

The kitchen door was open, so he walked straight in. Angela was sitting at her kitchen table at her computer. She looked up when she saw Hamish and gave a sigh of relief, pushing a wisp of hair out of her eyes.

"I can't get on with this book, Hamish," she complained. "When the first one was published, I thought I was all set. But the words won't come."

"Maybe you're trying too hard."

"Maybe. Let's have coffee."

Angela's first novel had been published the previous autumn. Reviews were good, but sales were modest.

"The trouble is I am damned as a 'literary writer,' " said Angela, "which usually means praise and no money."

"Perhaps something in the village will spark your imagination," said Hamish, covertly shooing two of her cats off the table where they were trying to drink the milk out of the jug.

"Like what?"

"Like this artist fellow. Seems to be a big hit with the ladies."

"Oh, he jokes and teases them. But I can't see anyone falling for him."

"Why?"

"In a funny kind of way, there's nothing about him that gives any of them the come-on. He's just a thoroughly nice man."

"Painting any good?"

"He's just started, but I looked his name up on the Internet. He's considered to be a very good landscape painter. He paints pictures in the old-fashioned way, and

16

people are going for that. I think they're moving away from elephant dung and unmade beds or whatever the modern artist has been exhibiting at the Tate. I don't think he's going to cause any dramas. Where are your animals?"

"I left them playing in the garden."

"Don't you find it odd that a dog and a wild cat should get on so well?"

"Not really. A relief, if you ask me. If Lugs hadn't taken to the cat, I'd need to have got rid of it."

"Be careful, Hamish. It is a wild cat, and they can be savage."

"I don't think there's such a thing as a pure wild cat any more. They've been interbreeding with the domestic ones for years. When I found Sonsie up on the moors with a broken leg, I didn't think the beast would live. Someone had been mistreating that animal. I'd dearly like to find out who it was."

"Maybe it just got caught in a trap."

"I've a feeling Sonsie had been kept captive somewhere."

"Here's your coffee. Is Effie Garrard still around?"

"Yes. I visited her the other day and asked around about her. Patel is selling her stuff, and so is the gift shop up at the

17

Tommel Castle Hotel. She does charge awfy high prices."

"Are you going to the ceilidh on Saturday?"

"I might drop in."

"You'll need a ticket. Five pounds."

"Five pounds! What on earth for?"

"The church hall needs repainting."

"I thought some of the locals would have done that for free."

"Oh, they are. But it's to raise money for repairs to the roof, paint, and new curtains."

"And what would I be getting for five pounds?"

"A buffet supper. The Italian restaurant is doing the catering."

"That's decent of them. I'll go."

"You must be getting very bored," said Angela, putting a mug of coffee in front of him. "No crime."

"And that just suits me fine. No crime now and no crime on the horizon."

Effie Garrard was a fantasist. Dreams were as essential to her as breathing. While Hamish sat in the doctor's wife's kitchen drinking coffee, Effie approached the village of Lochdubh, wrapped in a dream of attending her own funeral. Villagers wept,

18

the piper played a lament, famous artists came from all over to give their eulogies. She had decided to walk instead of taking her car because the day was so fine. The twin mountains behind the village soared up to a clear blue sky. Little glassy waves on the sea loch made a pleasant plashing sound as they curled onto the shingly beach.

A pleasurable tear ran down Effie's cheek, and she was wondering just how long she could stretch out this splendid dream when she saw Jock at his easel.

Her dream bubble burst as she experienced a jealous pang. She wanted to be the only artist in Lochdubh. Probably some amateur, she thought, approaching him. Jock's coterie of admiring women had left for dinner — dinner in Lochdubh still being in the middle of the day, except in posh places like the Tommel Castle Hotel.

Effie stood behind him and studied his work. His colours were magnificent. He had caught the purplish green of the forestry trees on the other side of the loch, and the reflections in the glassy loch had been painted by the hand of a master.

She did not want to interrupt him, but he turned round and smiled at her. "Grand day," said Jock.

"Oh, please go on. I'm an artist myself, and I hate to be interrupted," said Effie.

"I don't mind. I was just about to take a break. What do you do?"

"Small pictures of birds and flowers, and I'm a potter as well." She held out her hand. "Effie Garrard."

"I'm Jock Fleming. Wait a bit. I saw some of your pottery at the gift shop up at the hotel. You're very talented."

"Thank you. I live up in the hills above the village. Drop in on me any time you like."

"I'll do that."

Jock smiled at her again.

Effie gazed up at him in a dazed way. "Come now," she said.

"Can't. I promised the policeman I'd drop in for a dram."

"I know Hamish. I'll come with you."

"Not this time. It's man's talk. But I'll see you around."

Effie retreated, cursing herself. She had been too pushy. But she would act differently the next time. And, oh, there would be a next time. She hardly noticed the walk home. This time she was at her own wedding with Jock at her side. The church bells rang out over Lochdubh, and the villagers threw rose petals. "I loved you that

20

first moment I saw you," Jock murmured.

"Oh, it's yourself," said Hamish, letting Jock into the kitchen. "Where's your stuff?"

"In my car."

"You surely didnae drive the few yards from Mrs. Dunne's?"

"No, but it's a good place to put my paints when I'm taking a break."

"Sit down," said Hamish. "I'll get the whisky out."

Jock looked around the kitchen. It was a narrow room with cupboards and fridge along one wall and a wood-burning stove, which was sending out a blast of heat.

"I'm surprised you've got the fire on today," said Jock.

"It's got a back boiler. I'm heating up water for a shower."

"Wouldn't it be easier to have an immersion heater?"

"Thae things cost a mint." Hamish put a bottle of whisky, a jug of water, and two glasses on the table. "Besides, it'll be a long time afore we see a summer like this again."

He poured out two measures. "Water?"

"Just a splash."

Hamish sat down opposite him.

"Where are your animals?" asked Jock.

"Somewhere around," said Hamish, who had no intention of telling his visitor that the dog and the cat had eaten well and were now stretched out on his bed. The Currie sisters had started telling him he was behaving like an old maid. Even Archie Macleod had commented the other day that it looked as if Hamish was married to his dog and cat.

"How's the painting going?" asked Hamish.

"It was going fine until I got interrupted by a pushy woman."

"Mrs. Wellington, the minister's wife?"

"No, another artist. Effie Garrard."

"That quiet wee thing. I'd never have thought of her as being pushy."

"Oh, maybe I'm being hard on the woman."

"How pushy?" asked Hamish with his usual insatiable highland curiosity.

"Let me see. She asked me to drop in on her any time. Then she wanted me to go back with her there and then. I said I was coming to see you, and she said she would come as well. I told her it was man talk and got rid of her."

"Maybe she's lonelier than I thought," said Hamish.

Jock laughed. "You underrate my charms."

"I believe you're pretty well known. More whisky?"

"Just a little," said Jock. "My agent's coming up from Glasgow."

"I didn't know artists had agents."

"Well, we do. She takes her cut and finds me a gallery for an exhibition, and the gallery takes fifty percent. I used to do it myself until she found me and offered her services."

"How long do you think you'll stay up here?"

"I don't know. The light is fascinating, like nowhere else. I hope the good weather holds so I can make the most of it."

For the next two days, Effie found she could not concentrate on anything. She sat by the front window, looking down the brae to Lochdubh from early morning until late at night, waiting to see if Jock would call.

On the morning of the third day, she found that all her colourful dreams were beginning to get as thin as gossamer. This time she drove down in her little Ford Escort, not wanting to waste time walking, suddenly anxious to see him.

Jock was sitting at his easel, talking animatedly to Angela Brodie and Freda Campbell, the schoolteacher. Both were married, thought Effie sourly, and should be with their husbands. Freda was not long married, too, and to that local reporter, Matthew Campbell.

She waited patiently in her car for them to go. Then Jock began to pack up his things. Effie watched in dismay as they all headed for Angela's cottage.

She sat nervously biting her thumb.

At last, she got out of her car and went to Angela's cottage. The kitchen door was standing open, and she could hear the sounds of laughter. Squaring her small shoulders, she marched straight into the kitchen. Three startled pairs of eyes turned in her direction.

"Hullo, Jock," said Effie, ignoring the other two.

"Hullo. What can I do for you?"

"I've got some paintings and would like your opinion. Can you come up and see them?"

"I'm just about to get back to work," said Jock, getting to his feet. "Thanks for the company, ladies."

Effie followed him, practically running to keep up with his long strides. "What

24

about this evening?" she panted.

"Oh, all right," said Jock. "I'll be up at six. I'm meeting friends for dinner."

She gave him directions and then asked, "What friends?"

"Run along, Effie. I'll see you later."

For the rest of that day, Effie scrubbed and dusted until her cottage was shining. She took a bath in the brown peaty water that always came out of the taps and then dressed in a white wool dress and black velvet jacket. For the first time in her life, she wished she had some make-up. She had never worn any before, claiming it blocked up the pores.

Then she sat by the window. At five minutes past six, she was beginning to despair when she saw his car bumping and lurching over the heathery track that led to her cottage.

She flung open the door and stood beaming a welcome.

Jock ducked his head and followed her in. "Now, where are these paintings of yours?" he said.

"I thought you might like a glass of whisky first."

"I'm pressed for time."

Effie had laid out a selection of her small

framed paintings on the table. "Here they are," she said.

He picked one up and took it to the window and held it up to the light. "I'm surprised you can do anything in here," he said. "There isn't enough light."

The painting was of a thrush sitting on a branch of berries. The red of the berries glowed.

"This is exquisite," said Jock. "You're very good indeed."

Effie blushed with pleasure.

Jock appeared to have relaxed. He admired painting after painting and then her pieces of pottery. "Do you have an agent?" he asked. "These are much too good just to be shown in Patel's and the gift shop."

"No, I don't have one."

"My agent, Betty, will be here soon on holiday. I'll bring her along, if you like."

"Oh, Jock, that would be marvellous." She had moved so close to him she was practically leaning against his side.

He felt uneasy. "I've got to go, but I'll let you know when Betty arrives."

Jock made for the door. "Where are you having dinner?" asked Effie.

"The Tommel Castle Hotel. Bye."

He walked out to his car. He stopped for a moment and breathed in deep lungfuls of air. Then he got in and drove off.

Jock was not meeting anyone for dinner. But he decided to treat himself to dinner at the hotel.

He entered the dining room. A beautiful blonde approached him and said, "Have you come for dinner?"

"Yes."

"We've one table left," said the vision. "Thank goodness the tourists are back."

"You're a very glamorous maître d'," commented Jock.

"I'm standing in this evening. My parents run this hotel. I'm Priscilla Halburton-Smythe. Our maître d' is off sick."

She handed him a large menu and said, "Your waiter will be along in a minute. Would you like a drink?"

"No thanks. I'll order wine with the meal."

He watched Priscilla as she walked away. What a figure! And that beautiful bell of golden hair that framed her face! There was a remoteness about her which quickened his senses.

He made his meal last, watching while the other diners gradually finished theirs, hoping all the time for another few words with the beauty.

His back was to the window. At one point, he had an uneasy feeling of being watched. He turned round quickly, but there was no one there.

Priscilla at last came into the dining room and approached him. "Would you like anything else?"

"I would like you to join me for a coffee."

Priscilla looked amused. "I've just been hearing about you. You're Jock Fleming." She sat in a chair opposite him.

"Are you always here?" asked Jock.

"I work in London. I came up yesterday on holiday. I usually fill in for any of the missing staff when I'm here. It's a duty holiday to see my parents, and I find it can get a bit boring if I have nothing to do."

"I'd like to take you out one evening," said Jock. "Just friends," he added quickly, suddenly noticing she was wearing an engagement ring. "Where is your fiancé?"

"In London."

"So what do you say? What about tomorrow night at that Italian place?"

"All right," said Priscilla with a laugh. "What time?"

"Eight o'clock suit you?"

"Fine. Now I'd better go and see how they're getting on clearing up the kitchen."

Outside, Effie scuttled off from her observation post in the bushes opposite the dining room. Who was that woman? Perhaps she was Jock's agent. She would need to find out.

CHAPTER TWO

A dream itself is but a shadow.
— William Shakespeare

Priscilla had appeared in Lochdubh at the end of Hamish's last case and then had disappeared again like the mountain mist. If he thought of her — which he told himself was hardly ever — he decided it would be a long time before she ever came back.

They had been engaged at one time, and Hamish had broken off the engagement. There was a sexual coldness and distance about Priscilla that had been too hurtful to bear. And yet he had not found any other woman with whom he could fall so passionately in love as he had done with Priscilla.

He may have considered his emotions free of her, but the residents of Lochdubh did not, and so no one told him she was back at the hotel.

It was another lovely day, and he was

tempted to skip going on his rounds, which covered more and more miles each year as the government shut down other local police stations. But duty was duty, and some of the old folk in the outlying crofts might have fallen ill. He got in the police Land Rover and set off, taking his dog and cat with him.

There was a new softness to the air. Hamish guessed there was some rain coming. The water in the loch had changed to light grey, although the sky was still blue and the mountains appeared very close, each cleft and rock as distinct as in a steel engraving.

At one point in the afternoon, he parked up on the moors and took out a packed lunch he had brought with him along with food for the dog and cat. He sat down in the heather and fed the animals and himself.

All at once, he had a sudden sharp feeling that Priscilla was near, but he dismissed it from his mind. If she were back in Lochdubh, someone would have told him.

Down on the waterfront, Mrs. Wellington, large and tweedy and wearing a brown velvet hat with a pheasant's feather stuck in it, hailed Angela Brodie.

31

"Have you told Hamish that Miss Halburton-Smythe is up at the hotel?"

"I've only just learned of her arrival," said Angela. "I went to the police station to tell him, but he was out."

"We're not going to tell him," said Mrs. Wellington, waving a plump arm which seemed to encompass the whole village.

"Why not? He's bound to find out sooner or later."

"We think the reason he's never married is because he's still hankering after her."

"But that's no reason to treat him like a child."

"We don't want him getting hurt. With any luck, she'll be off back to London before he knows anything about it."

Effie was dressing with extreme care for the ceilidh that evening. She dreamed of dancing with Jock, of him holding her close and whispering into her hair that he loved her. She had bought a white cotton dress and a tartan sash in Strathbane. "I look the very picture of a highland lass," she told her reflection. She had also bought make-up for the first time in her life. She sat down at her dressing table she had hardly ever used, and applied the foundation cream and then powder. She painted her lips with a scarlet lipstick and then surveyed the effect with pleasure. "I look about nineteen," she told her reflection.

Jock Fleming, dressed in his one good suit, collar, and tie, walked into the Italian restaurant and was ushered to a table by Willie Lamont, the waiter.

"I'm waiting for someone," said Jock. "I'll choose what to eat when she arrives. Ah, here she is now."

Priscilla was wearing jeans, a cotton shirt belted at the waist, and low-heeled sandals. Jock suddenly felt overdressed.

Then he realised the other diners in the restaurant had fallen silent.

After Priscilla had sat down, he said, "We seem to be attracting a great deal of attention."

"You're new here," said Priscilla easily, "and still a subject of gossip."

"But they're not gossiping. They're staring."

"Ignore them." Priscilla picked up the menu.

"Am I overdressed?" asked Jock.

"I forgot to tell you. There's a ceilidh in the church hall tonight. I thought we would go along afterwards. I'm surprised there's so many in here. The restaurant is supplying a buffet supper at the ceilidh."

The mystery was solved when Willie approached to take their order and asked if they had tickets for the ceilidh.

"Why?" asked Priscilla. "I've never needed a ticket before."

"It's like this," said Willie. "It's a set meal here tonight which is covered by the ceilidh ticket because the restaurant is supplying the eats at the hall. If you've got a ticket, you don't pay here and I mark your ticket that you've been fed."

"We haven't got tickets," said Jock impatiently. "We'll just choose from the menu." He opened the menu and found it contained a single sheet of typed paper. On it was written three courses: salad, lasagne, and chocolate mousse.

"You can't have anything if you haven't got tickets," said Willie.

Jock raised his bushy eyebrows in despair.

"Get us two tickets, and we'll pay for them," said Priscilla patiently.

"Wine's extra," cautioned Willie.

"Just get the tickets, Willie."

Willie went away and came back with two tickets. Jock paid for them and said, "This is a madhouse."

"Never mind. We don't need to bother

choosing anything, as it's all been chosen for us. How are you enjoying your stay?"

"Very much. I'm being pestered a bit, though, by Effie Garrard."

"Our gift shop sells her stuff. She's very, very good."

"I'll grant you that. Maybe she's just lonely. Don't you find it too quiet up here after London?"

"I was brought up here."

"And will you live in London when you are married?"

"Yes, my fiancé's work is there."

"When's the wedding?"

A shadow crossed Priscilla's face. "Peter, my fiancé, is waiting until he can get a good break from work."

"I would think any man in his right mind wouldn't leave you loose for long."

Willie appeared behind Jock. "Would you like to examine the kitchen?"

"No, I wouldn't," said Jock crossly.

"Just for a minute."

"Go away, Willie," said Priscilla.

Willie retreated.

"What was all that about?" asked Jock.

"Oh, you'll find out sooner or later. I was once engaged to Hamish Macbeth."

"The policeman?"

"Yes. He broke off the engagement, but I

35

fear the villagers still hope we'll get together again."

"But they know you are engaged?"

"Of course. But they prefer to ignore it."

"Odd place, this. It all seems so calm and unruffled on the surface, and underneath there seems to be all sorts of things going on. Why did Hamish break off the engagement?"

"Mind your own business," said Priscilla coolly, "and tell me about yourself."

So Jock did, telling her about his early days at Glasgow School of Art and his struggles to make a living as a painter.

"And you can do that now?" asked Priscilla.

"Yes, I'm pretty successful, thanks to my agent, Betty Barnard. Terrific energy that woman has. She worked night and day until she found me a gallery."

Their food arrived. Jock ordered wine. They chatted amiably as the restaurant cleared of customers.

"That was very pleasant," said Priscilla when they finished.

"I don't usually do portraits, but I would like to do one of you."

"What! Sit on the waterfront, which is where I gather from the gossips that you do your painting?"

"I was hoping you might lend me somewhere in the hotel."

"I'll think about it. Let's go."

Jock and Priscilla entered the hall to a roll of drums. "Take your seats, ladies and gentlemen," announced Matthew Campbell, the reporter who had been elected master of ceremonies. "Lochdubh's very own line dancing team will entertain you."

Jock tried hard not to laugh. The Currie sisters, Mrs. Wellington, Freda, Angela, and various other village women in what they fondly thought was western dress cavorted to a rollicking country and western tune played on the fiddle and accordion.

His eyes were streaming with suppressed laughter by the time they finished. Then Matthew announced, "And now take your partners for a ladies' choice. It's the eightsome reel."

Effie rushed up to Jock. "Our dance, I think," she said.

"I don't know how to do it."

"Come on. We'll just follow the others."

Hamish walked over and sat down by Priscilla. "You might have told me you had arrived," he said.

"I was going to call on you tomorrow.

37

Oh, do look at Effie and Jock. They're falling over everyone."

"You came in with Jock?"

"Yes, he took me for dinner."

Hamish was suddenly and jealously glad Jock was making such a mess of things. He blundered into people in his set and finally sent Jessie Currie flying.

"You know," said Priscilla, "for an artist, Effie does have a clumsy hand with make-up. She looks like a clown."

Effie's make-up was dead white, and she had tried to make her small mouth look larger. She had set her hair in tight curls.

"Looks like Ronald McDonald," said Hamish, who was gradually falling into a nasty mood. There was Priscilla as calm, as seemingly *indifferent,* as ever.

"Have you got a day off tomorrow?" asked Priscilla.

"Yes. Why?"

"I'll take us out on a picnic, and we can catch up on the gossip."

Hamish's face cleared. "Great. Mind you, I smell rain."

"If it rains, we can go down to Strathbane. There's a new French restaurant opened. It's down at the docks."

"What a place to have a restaurant."

"It's part of the regeneration of that area.

38

Anyone who sets up business gets a tax break."

Jock came back to join them, and to his dismay, Effie followed and sat down beside him.

Gamekeeper Henry was then called to the stage to recite a poem. After him, a little girl in a tutu tried to perform steps from *Swan Lake*, fell over, and burst into tears.

The next dance was a St. Bernard's waltz. Priscilla and Hamish rose as one person and went on to the floor.

"Shall we?" asked Effie, and Jock did not have the courage to refuse. The steps were simple, and they managed very well, although Jock did not like the way Effie pressed up against him.

After the dance was over, she said she was going to the ladies'. Jock walked quickly to the door of the church hall and made his way outside. A fine heavy rain was soaking the waterfront.

Jock put up his collar and hurried back to his boarding house. He was still determined to paint Priscilla and see if he could find out what really lay behind that calm mask.

To Hamish's delight, the rain cleared on the following morning. He phoned Angela and asked her to keep an eye on his animals, showered, and got ready to drive up to the hotel and meet Priscilla. They would be taking her car because he didn't want his day spoiled by someone reporting that he was driving a civilian around in the police Land Rover. Not that anyone in Lochdubh would do such a thing, but his beat now covered Cnothan, a sour town, where several of the inhabitants would be delighted if they thought they could put in a complaint about him.

He was about to leave when the phone rang. He hesitated on the doorstep. What if it was something important? But what if it were some minor complaint that might still ruin his day off?

The answering machine picked it up, and he heard Priscilla's voice. He rushed and picked up the receiver. "It's me, Hamish."

"Hamish, I'll need to cancel our picnic."

"Why?"

"Mrs. Tullet, who runs the gift shop on Sundays, has a bad stomach complaint. I'll need to take over."

"Can't someone else do it? I mean, if you weren't there, someone would have to."

"Mother would probably do it, but she

has asked me to fill in."

"What about this evening? We could drive down to that French restaurant you were talking about."

"Not this evening, Hamish. Some other time. Got to go."

Hamish slowly replaced the receiver. The day now stretched out before him, bleak and empty. At the best of times, there was a sad, closed air about a highland Sabbath as if the ghosts of Calvin and John Knox still haunted the place, determined to make sure no one was enjoying themselves.

He phoned Angela and told her his outing had been cancelled, and then he set out to walk along the waterfront with the dog and the cat at his heels.

He saw a stranger approaching, a tall woman wearing a tailored trouser suit. She had thick brown hair with gold highlights and a strong, handsome face.

"Good morning," said Hamish politely. "Grand day."

"Yes, I've been lucky with the weather."

"Are you staying up at the hotel?"

"Yes, I'm Betty Barnard, Jock Fleming's agent. I've found a gallery for Jock in Glasgow, so I've just been to see him. I'm sending him off for a couple of weeks."

"I'm Hamish Macbeth. Are you going with him?"

"No need. I've done the groundwork. I'm really in need of a holiday, but if there's anything urgent, I can cope with it by e-mail. Those are two very odd . . ."

"Animals," said Hamish grumpily. "I know. I'm tired of talking about them."

She had very large green eyes. Hamish reflected that it wasn't often one saw eyes as green as hers. Might be contact lenses.

She leaned against the waterfront wall, and Hamish joined her. "Is this your day off?"

"Yes. I was going to go on a picnic with a friend, but she cancelled."

"Pity. Tell you what. I'll go back to the hotel and get them to fix up two packed lunches, and then we could go on a picnic and you can introduce me to the area."

She exuded an easy-going friendliness. She was somewhere in her early forties, Hamish guessed, with an attractive husky voice. Her mouth was generous, and she had a determined chin.

"That's very kind of you," said Hamish. "But we'll need to take your car. I can't drive civilians in the police car."

"Fine. I'll see you in half an hour." As she walked away to where her car was parked, she turned around. "You can bring your dog and cat."

Well, thought Hamish with a rush of gladness, it's going to be a good day, after all.

Effie marched determinedly towards Sea View, where Jock had a room. In her fantasies, she had decided the artist was shy under his bluff, easy-going manner. He needed a bit of encouragement.

But as she approached, she saw to her dismay that Jock was lifting a suitcase into the boot of his car.

"Are you leaving?" she asked, running up to him.

"Just for a couple of weeks. There's a gallery I've got to see." He slammed down the boot and went to get into the driving seat.

"Jock," said Effie boldly, putting one small hand on his arm, "do you ever think of getting married?"

He looked down at her intense face and felt a sudden rush of sympathy for her. Poor wee woman, he thought. Life must be lonely for her up here.

"I'm not the marrying kind, Effie. But if I did get married, it would be to someone like you." He gave her a kiss on the cheek, got into his car, slammed the door, and roared off.

Effie stood, watching him go, her hand to her cheek and her spirits soaring. Her brain deleted the "not the marrying kind" bit. Surely that had been a proposal. And he'd kissed her!

Priscilla looked out of the gift shop window just at the moment when Hamish was getting into Betty Barnard's car. Hamish even had his dog and his cat with him. Betty drove off. She was laughing at something Hamish was saying.

Mr. Johnson, the hotel manager, came into the shop. "I've just seen Hamish driving off with that Barnard woman," said Priscilla.

"Yes, Miss Barnard ordered a couple of packed lunches."

Priscilla fiddled nervously with a strand of her hair. "He was supposed to go with me for a picnic."

"And why didn't he?"

"I was needed here."

"You should have told me. I could have got one of the women from the village to fill in. They'd have been glad of the money."

"Well, it's too late now. I wonder how they met."

44

"She probably picked Hamish up. He's an attractive man."

"Is there anything in particular you wanted to talk to me about?" asked Priscilla sharply.

"No, just checking you were all right."

After he had left, Priscilla went to serve a customer. She had been glad of an excuse not to go out with Hamish. She did not want any of her old feelings for him coming back. But trust Hamish to immediately get a date with the only attractive woman around!

Effie was sitting wrapped in dreams when there was a knock at the door. She found the Currie sisters standing there.

"What?" she asked rudely.

"We came to ask if you would like to give some pottery classes to the Mothers' Union," said Nessie.

"Union," echoed Jessie, who always repeated the end of her sister's sentences.

"I'm afraid I am too busy."

"We've walked all the way here," said Nessie. "Aren't you going to invite us in?"

"Invite us in?" said Jessie. "Us in?"

Effie suddenly saw a way of establishing Jock as her property in the village minds. "I'm afraid I've got a gentleman with me.

It's Jock. I'm afraid you're interrupting."

"Such carryings-on and this the Sabbath, too," said Nessie.

"Sabbath, too!" exclaimed her sister.

They both turned and scurried off.

When they reached the waterfront, the first person they saw was Mrs. Dunne, the proprietor of Sea View. Mrs. Dunne listened patiently to their shocked exclamations and then said patiently, "Herself must have just wanted rid of you. Jock Fleming left earlier today. And, no, he couldnae have done a detour because Henry, the gamekeeper, saw him heading off down towards Lairg."

Hamish Macbeth returned to the police station that evening feeling happy and relaxed. He had enjoyed a pleasant day. He had guided Betty round all the local beauty spots. She had really endeared herself to him when it transpired that she had brought along food for the dog and cat as well. Hamish did not know it was Clarry, the hotel chef and a friend of his, who had thoughtfully added the food in two packets, one labelled Lugs and the other Sonsie.

He looked forward to seeing Betty again. He checked his messages. No crime. It was going to be a great summer.

Effie, the next day, began to fret about
Priscilla. Jock had taken her for dinner.
Effie was anxious to impress upon women
in general and Priscilla in particular that
Jock was her property.

Her obsession was at boiling point.
Nothing was going to stand in her way. She
got into her car and drove down to
Strathbane to a shop which sold second-
hand rings. She bought herself a diamond
engagement ring. Such was her obsession
when she drove back that she could almost
believe that Jock had given it to her.

But they would laugh about it after they
were married.

Effie knew that there was to be a sale of
work by the Mothers' Union at the church
the next day. That would be a good place
to start.

And that was to be the day when
Hamish Macbeth's peaceful summer came
to an abrupt end.

The first call Hamish got the following
morning was to tell him to get over to
Braikie, where a gunman was holding
people hostage in the Highland and
Sutherland Bank.

The bane of his life, Detective Chief Inspector Blair, snarled down the phone. "Just you secure the area. A team of us are on the way, and we've got a proper hostage negotiator."

Villagers turned and stared as the police Land Rover sped off through the village with the blue light flashing and the siren blaring.

Hamish arrived in the main street of Braikie. A woman was standing crying, surrounded by a group of people. "She just got oot o' there in time," said one man.

Hamish went up to her. "Tell me what happened," he asked.

She gulped and said, "I work there as a teller. I was late for the morning shift because my bairn wasn't feeling well. I had to wait to get someone to look after her. I opened the door of the bank, saw a gunman and people lying on the floor, and backed out. It's awful!"

Hamish took her name and address. "Is there a back door to the bank?"

"Aye, it's got a little kitchen where we make the morning coffee."

"Don't any of you move," said Hamish, "and make sure everyone keeps clear of the bank until reinforcements arrive."

Hamish found himself getting very angry

indeed. A bank robbery! In the Highlands! And on his beat!

He went to his Land Rover and took out a small tool kit. He went round and surveyed the back door. There was a glass pane on it, but the pane was protected by heavy metal bars. The door hinges were on the outside, however. He took out a screwdriver and a can of oil. He squirted oil on the hinges and got to work with the screwdriver, working furiously until he was able to lift the door off its hinges. There was an alarm above the door, but it didn't go off. Probably hadn't been serviced in years, he thought.

He took off his boots and went in quietly in his stockinged feet. He gently opened the door that led into the main floor of the small bank. A terrified girl was stuffing banknotes into a sack while a man on the other side of the counter held a sawn-off shotgun on her.

It was an old-fashioned bank. There was no bulletproof glass screen between the teller and the customer, only a mahogany counter which sloped up to the teller and down on the teller's side.

Hamish took out his telescopic truncheon, sprang across the floor, and vaulted over the counter, driving his feet straight into the gunman's chest. The gunman fell backwards, and the shotgun went off, blasting a hole in the ceiling.

Hamish smashed the truncheon down on the arm holding the shotgun.

"You've broke my arm," screamed the gunman.

Hamish flipped him over and handcuffed him. Then he wrenched off the balaclava hiding the man's face. It was a face he didn't recognise, and he was glad of that. He had been afraid it might be one of the locals and had not liked to think that one of them had decided to go in for bank robbery.

From outside the bank, Blair's unlovely Glaswegian voice sounded through a loud-hailer. "You are surrounded. You cannot escape. Come out with your hands up."

The townspeople were now crowded behind police barriers.

The door of the bank opened, and Hamish Macbeth appeared, pushing the handcuffed gunman in front of him.

A great cheer went up from the crowd.

Blair's face darkened in anger. A local cameraman was busy taking pictures. Police took the gunman off to a waiting police van.

The bank manager, looking white and

shaken, came out in time to hear Blair raging at Hamish, "You should have waited. I have a trained negotiator here."

The bank manager, Mr. Queen, said crossly, "If it hadn't been for Hamish, some of us might have been killed. There'll be a reward for you, Hamish."

A policeman came up and said, "There's a call from Mrs. Sutherland's store in Cnothan. She's caught a shoplifter."

Blair's face cleared. Here was a way to get the triumphant Macbeth off the scene before any more press arrived.

"That's your beat," he said. "Hop to it."

"What about my statement?" asked Hamish.

"You can send it in later. Off you go."

And so Hamish headed off to Cnothan, unaware of the fuss and gossip Effie was causing at the sale of work.

Chapter Three

*Thou are gone from my gaze like a
beautiful dream,
And I seek thee in vain by the meadow
and stream.*
— George Linley

The members of the Mothers' Union were inclined to snub Effie, each one feeling she might have offered to help the cause by putting some of her own work up for sale.

Effie, complete with garish make-up, cruised the stalls, picking up things and putting them back. Then as she stopped in front of Mrs. Wellington's stall, which was full of all the unsuccessful junk recycled from the last sale, she picked up a horrible green vase. A shaft of sunlight struck down through the grimy windows and sparkled on the diamond ring on her engagement finger.

"Is that an engagement ring?" boomed Mrs. Wellington.

The chatter in the hall suddenly died.

"Indeed it is," said Effie with a smile.

"And who is the lucky fellow?"

"Jock Fleming," said Effie triumphantly.

All the women crowded around her as Effie beamed in triumph. In that heady moment, she was sure Jock had actually bought her the ring.

"When did he pop the question?" asked Angela.

"Just before he left."

"So when's the wedding?" asked Freda, who was visiting the sale of work on her lunch break.

"As soon as we can," said Effie. "Jock is so impetuous."

"I never would ha' thought it," murmured one woman.

Effie heard her and scowled. "It was a whirlwind romance," she said loudly.

Angela looked at the little defiant figure of Effie with her clown's make-up and felt a pang of unease.

Maybe Hamish Macbeth knew more about it than she did.

Hamish had just finished sending over his report about the attempted bank robbery when Angela knocked at the kitchen door. He had not sent a report about the shoplifting because the culprits turned out to be two small terrified schoolchildren who had stolen a chocolate bar each. Hamish had spent a weary afternoon persuading the angry shopkeeper not to press charges, then delivered the sobbing children to their respective parents.

"Come in, Angela," he said.

"Have you heard the news about Effie?"

"What news?"

"She's flashing around a diamond ring saying she's engaged to Jock. Hamish, she looked quite mad, and her make-up is worse than ever. Do you think it's true?"

"I don't know. I'd have thought it highly unlikely. I'll go and call on her."

Effie answered her cottage door to Hamish. She had scrubbed off the dreadful make-up and looked perfectly sane to Hamish.

"I called to congratulate you," said Hamish.

"How kind. Come in."

Hamish removed his cap and followed her into her living-room-cum-kitchen-cum-studio.

"When did all this happen?"

"Just as Jock was leaving. He said he couldn't live without me."

Hamish conjured up a picture of easy-going Jock in his mind. "Are you sure you didn't misunderstand him?" he asked cautiously.

Her face flamed with anger. "He gave me this ring! Now, go!"

Hamish eased towards the door. He looked down at the work table. There was a jug full of paintbrushes, but they looked hard and dry, and he could swear the pottery wheel had a film of dust on it.

"I see you haven't been working," he said.

"Of course I have, and I'd like to get on with some more. Go away!"

And Hamish left, a very worried man. Newcomers had meant trouble in the past, and somewhere inside him, he could feel bad times coming.

As he drove back to the police station, thin wisps of black clouds were sweeping in from the Atlantic, as if in keeping with his mood.

He gave a mental shrug. He was worrying too much. If Jock had asked Effie to marry him, then his agent would know about it. He swung the steering wheel and headed for the Tommel Castle Hotel.

Priscilla was crossing the reception area

when Hamish entered the hotel. "Why, Hamish, what brings you here?"

"I want to see Betty Barnard."

"She was out for a walk, and now I think she's in the bar."

"Thanks."

Hamish strode off in the direction of the bar, leaving Priscilla staring after him.

Betty was ensconced in a corner by the window with a book and a glass of whisky.

She looked up as he approached. "Hamish, what a nice surprise."

"Mind if I join you?"

"Not at all. I was thinking of phoning you."

"My treat next time. What I was wondering was whether you knew anything about this business about Jock going to marry Effie."

"Who the hell . . . ?"

"Effie Garrard. An artist who lives here. She's flashing around an engagement ring and says Jock is going to marry her."

"Jock is divorced and swore blind he'd never marry again. Is this Effie beautiful?"

"No. She was at the ceilidh. Wait a bit. You weren't there."

"Nobody asked me."

"I should have done," said Hamish ruefully. "She seemed to be chasing Jock, and he looked as if he didn't like it one bit."

"I'll look into it. Where does she live?"

"Not going to have a row or anything?"

"Why should I? Jock's a valued client, but that's all. But I am protective of my clients."

Hamish gave her directions and then said, "There's another odd thing. Although she's been supplying art works for sale, the pottery wheel has dust on it and her paintbrushes are dry and stiff."

"Aha! Meaning you think she's been getting the stuff from somewhere else and passing it off as her own?"

"Just a thought."

"Leave her to me."

Betty drove up to Effie's cottage. Effie answered the door. "Who are you?"

"I'm Jock's agent, Betty Barnard. May I come in?"

"Just for a moment."

Betty walked in and looked around, her sharp eyes taking in the details Hamish had noticed.

She turned and faced Effie. "What's this rubbish about you and Jock getting married?"

"It's not rubbish. It's the truth. Look!" Effie waved the diamond ring under Betty's nose.

"When did he propose?"

"Just before he left."

"I don't believe it. Jock swore he would never get married again."

"Well, believe it and get out of here."

Betty turned in the doorway and said, "I don't believe you're an artist, either. No artist would leave paintbrushes like that, and the pottery wheel looks as if it hasn't been used."

"You bitch!" screamed Effie. "I'm an artist, and I'll get Jock to fire you as soon as he gets back!"

Betty gave a contemptuous shrug and walked out. Effie followed her, beside herself with rage.

"He'll need to marry me anyway," she shouted as Betty was getting into her car.

Betty swung round. "Why? What d'you mean?"

"I'm pregnant."

And with that bombshell, Effie went back in and slammed the door.

Betty phoned Hamish and asked him to meet her at the Italian restaurant for dinner.

He found her nervous and agitated. "Effie says Jock's got to marry her because she's pregnant," she burst out as soon as Hamish sat down.

"It might be possible," said Hamish. "Does he drink a lot?"

"He goes on binges from time to time."

"He could've got plastered and taken her to bed."

"I don't know."

"Have you phoned him?"

"I've tried. The gallery said he was staying with friends, and I don't have their number. I left a message for him to phone back, but he often doesn't reply for a couple of days, particularly if he's out partying with other artists."

"There's really nothing we can do until he gets in touch," said Hamish. "Order something and have some wine. I'm getting this."

Willie came to take their orders. "I saw Miss Halburton-Smythe today," he said. "Herself was looking as beautiful as ever."

"Take the orders and go away, Willie," snapped Hamish.

"Everyone seems to mind everyone else's business around here," said Betty after they had ordered. She glanced out of the window. "It looks as if rain is coming . . . Oh, my God. This is all Jock needs!"

"What?"

"I've just seen his ex-wife walking past."

"What's she doing here?"

"He's probably behind with the alimony as usual and she's hunting him down. Right little harpy."

"When did he get divorced?"

"Two years ago."

"Children?"

"Two. A boy and a girl."

"How old are they?"

"The boy, Callum, is six, and Shona, the girl, five."

"Why did the marriage break up?"

"I don't really know. Can we talk about something else? I've had enough of Jock and his problems for one evening."

The next day, Hamish was in Patel's general store when he saw Angela. Behind a stack of cans of baked beans — Lochdubh's favourite food — he said to her in a low voice, "There's a further complication. Effie is saying she's pregnant."

The Currie sisters, on the other side of the stack of baked beans, clutched each other. Then, forgetting their shopping, they hurried out to spread the news around the village about Effie's pregnancy.

The villagers warmed to Effie. Poor wee lassie. Getting knocked up like that. Of course, she was a bit old to be having a baby, but look at old Mrs. McClutcheon. She had got pregnant with her last when she was fifty! And so the gossip ran round and round.

Effie did experience moments of sheer dread on the odd occasions when reality returned. But Jock had said he would marry her, she thought, stubbornly rephrasing his last goodbye.

But as the rain continued to hammer down on the corrugated iron roof of her cottage until she thought the sound of it would drive her mad, she learned from Mrs. Wellington, who had called to bring her some scones, that Jock's ex-wife was in the village waiting for him.

"What's she like?" asked Effie.

"Small, blonde, and beautiful," said the minister's wife. "I wouldn't worry about it. Jock was obviously looking for quality of character this time round." And with that backhanded compliment, she took her leave.

Jealousy like bile rose up in Effie. Jock was hers, and she was going to keep him.

And then two days later, Jock Fleming came back bringing the good weather with him. Hamish saw him sitting at his easel on the waterfront and went to talk to him.

"Same old view?" commented Hamish.

"Different angle," said Jock.

"So are you going to marry Effie?"

"Don't be daft. I'll go and see her and sort that one out. She's mad."

"I'm glad that's over," said Hamish. "Have you seen your ex-wife?"

"Dora? Yes, she's staying at Sea View as well."

"That doesn't bother you?"

"No, we get on all right."

"Why did the marriage break up?"

"Hamish, run along. You're as nosy as the rest of them."

Hamish touched his cap and moved off. In that moment, he was sorry for Effie, probably sitting in her cottage with the ruin of her dreams tumbling about her ears. He thought of calling on her, but the lazy warm days were back and he had promised to go for a drive soon with Betty.

Hamish drove back to the police station two evenings later, happy and contented. He thought Betty was splendid company, and deep down he enjoyed the fact that Priscilla knew of his friendship with the agent.

He fed Sonsie and Lugs and took them out for a walk up the fields at the back of the station.

Detective Inspector Jimmy Anderson phoned to give Hamish a date for when the bank robber would be appearing at the sheriff's court. "He's got a list of offences as long as your arm," said Jimmy. "Name's Hugh McFarlane, all the way from Glasgow."

When Hamish rang off, it was to find Mrs. Wellington waiting for him. "I've been up to Effie's cottage," she said. "The door was unlocked, and I walked in when she didn't answer. No sign of her. Her car is there."

"She probably went for a walk," said Hamish.

"Do me a favour. Go up there and just check the place out. It isn't like the old days, you know. Nobody goes out any more and leaves their door unlocked."

Hamish took his cat and his dog with him. Although he was beginning to think that Effie was slightly mad, he thought that Mrs. Wellington was being over-fussy.

He went up to the cottage, opened the door, and called, "Effie!"

Silence.

He stepped inside. The main room was dark and deserted. Putting a handkerchief over his hand, he switched on the light.

The first thing he noticed was that the room had been scrubbed clean. He sniffed the air. There was a strong smell of cleaning fluid. He searched the kitchen and then went into the bedroom. The bed was made up, and Effie's clothes were in the wardrobe. On the bedside table was a framed photograph of Jock at his easel. Hamish took out a pair of latex gloves, put them on, and picked up the photograph. It looked like an amateur snapshot that had been enlarged. It was signed, "To my darling Effie. Jock."

Hamish replaced the photograph.

Perhaps Jock had been lying, and he really had proposed to Effie and was now trying to pretend it never happened.

The rain that had left Lochdubh alone for a few days had come back in force, and Hamish heard it hammering on the roof. How could she bear that noise?

He went out to the Land Rover, where Lugs and Sonsie were patiently waiting, took his oilskin out of the back, put it on, and began to search around the heathery fields outside the cottage, calling, "Effie!" from time to time.

He went back into the cottage to see if there was any clue he had missed. This time he saw an obvious one. At the side of the armchair by the fireplace was a handbag. Still wearing his gloves, he opened it up. Effie's wallet and change purse were there along with her door keys and car keys.

Now what to do? he wondered. If he reported her missing and started a full-scale and expensive search and she just came wandering back, he would look silly. He got back into the Land Rover to wait. The wind rose, and the rain became even heavier, lashing against the windscreen, great gusts rocking the vehicle.

At last, he decided something was really wrong and drove back to the police station. He phoned headquarters and asked for permission to call out the Mountain Rescue Patrol.

He was told to phone again in the morning, and if there was still no sighting of her, then the patrol would be alerted.

He fed himself and his animals and then phoned the minister and told him the situation and asked him to ring the church bell first thing in the morning. This would get the villagers gathered in the church hall, and he could organise a search party.

Hamish slept uneasily. He got up at dawn and went back to Effie's cottage. It was still deserted. The rain had ceased, and the sky had a pale, washed-out look as if a heavenly hand had scrubbed it clean.

At eight o'clock, after he had again phoned police headquarters and this time extracted a promise that the Mountain Rescue Patrol would be sent out immediately, he went to the church hall, where the villagers were gathering. He went up to the podium and addressed them.

"Effie Garrard is missing. She may have taken a walk up on the moors and had an accident. I want everyone who's free to help me in a search for her. The folks who are prepared to go stay in the hall."

Because of the storm, the fishing boats hadn't been out, and so Archie Macleod and his friends volunteered to join in the search along with the river bailiff and two gamekeepers from the Tommel Castle estate. Women, headed by Mrs. Wellington, volunteered as well.

Priscilla arrived just as the meeting was breaking up. "I've just heard," she said. "I'll go along with Mrs. Wellington."

They all gathered again outside Effie's cottage. Then they spread out over the moors, calling and searching.

Above them flew a helicopter of the Mountain Rescue Patrol.

All day long they searched without

finding Effie. Hamish began to worry that she had fallen into a peat bog, and if that were the case, they would never find her.

The villagers began to think that Effie had perhaps committed suicide. Jock had been adamant that he had never proposed to Effie.

The indomitable Mrs. Wellington with her posse of village women set out again the next day. It was glorious weather. They all drove up on the moors as far as the road would allow them and then got out of their vehicles and once more began the search, agreeing to meet again at midday for a picnic lunch.

Hamish came across them at noon. They were sitting by a little stream with their picnic spread out on the grass. "That one can smell free food a mile off," grumbled one, and Hamish flushed angrily.

Priscilla came up to him. "You look exhausted, Hamish. I've got a flask of coffee and some spare sandwiches. Come and sit down for a minute."

Hamish gratefully accepted a cup of coffee and a chicken sandwich. "You don't think she might have gone up into the mountains?" he said. "She must have been right distressed being caught out in that lie about Jock."

"I can't help feeling sorry for her. She's got a sister down in Brighton. Does anyone know her address?"

"No, but I phoned the Brighton police, and they're looking for her. I would have thought Effie might have gone there, but her handbag is still at the cottage."

Priscilla was wearing a tartan shirt, corduroy trousers, and sturdy boots but still managed to look cool and elegant.

"I thought Betty Barnard might have joined in the search," Hamish said.

"She's gone off to Glasgow for a few days. I don't suppose she even knows Effie is missing."

Gone and never even told me, thought Hamish gloomily. I have no luck with women at all.

Mrs. Wellington was armed with a powerful pair of Zeiss binoculars. "I'll just have a look around," she boomed, "and then we can start off again."

"It is hot," said Priscilla, "and yet Mrs. Wellington is wearing a Harris tweed suit with a sweater under it."

"I think that one carries around her own air conditioning," said Hamish. "Is there another sandwich?"

"Got one right here. There you are."

"I think I see something," called Mrs.

Wellington. "Right up on the mountain."

Hamish stood up and went to her. "Let me see."

She handed him the binoculars. "Up there, halfway up, by that cleft of rock. It was in the shadow when I looked before, but the sun's moved."

Hamish took the glasses and adjusted them. He focussed on the cleft. It looked like a small brown lump.

"I don't think so," he said, "but I'd better climb up there and have a look."

"I'll come with you," said Priscilla. "It'll take us at least two hours to get up there."

"That's Geordie's Cleft," said Hamish. It had been named after a young man who had fallen to his death some years before.

They set off, promising to holler if they found anything.

After they had gone, Mrs. Wellington tried to marshal her troops, but rebellion was setting in. The Currie sisters complained their legs were aching, and one by one the other village women began to edge back to their cars until only Mrs. Wellington and Angela Brodie remained.

Hamish and Priscilla kept up a gruelling pace as they climbed up the lower slopes of the mountain and then out onto the rock.

It was easier going than they had expected, a path leading upwards for most of the way.

"People have been up here before," said Hamish.

"There was a rumour a year ago that some of the village boys came up here to smoke pot," said Priscilla.

"And you never told me!"

"Didn't seem like a major crime, and at that time, you had a murder case on your hands."

The sun beat down on their backs as they approached the cleft. Two buzzards sailed lazily overhead.

"There's something there," said Hamish, "unless someone's dumped a bundle of old clothes."

But as he got nearer, his heart sank. The small figure of a woman was lying on her face.

He went up and, putting on his gloves, turned the body over. It was Effie Garrard. There was no sign of life.

Priscilla followed him. "How did she die?" she whispered.

"I don't know," said Hamish. "Exposure, maybe."

He took out his phone and called Mountain Rescue and then called police headquarters in Strathbane.

Priscilla went a little way away and sat down suddenly.

Hamish finished phoning. "Feeling sick?"

"Look at her hand, Hamish. The left hand."

Hamish bent down and let out a sharp exclamation.

Effie's ring finger had been sawn off.

CHAPTER FOUR

Father, O Father! what do we here
In this land of unbelief and fear?
The Land of Dreams is better far,
Above the light of the morning star.
— William Blake

Hamish told Priscilla to phone Mrs. Wellington to say that Effie had been found, but he ordered that no one except the police were to come near the site.

Priscilla moved a good bit away to sit down and stare blankly into space. Hamish began to check round about the body. Effie was lying on hard rock just outside the cleft, so he was not afraid of messing up any footprints.

He found a wine bottle not far from the body. He crouched down and sniffed. There was a sweetish smell, and squinting at the label, he could see it was a dessert wine.

Two helicopters landed down below the

mountain, and he saw the figures of police and members of the Mountain Rescue Patrol climbing down onto the heather.

First on the scene was Detective Jimmy Anderson. "Where's Blair?" asked Hamish.

"He's too fat to climb. He's sitting down there swigging whisky out of a flask. What have we got?"

"The dead woman is Effie Garrard, a local artist," said Hamish. "She had gone missing, and we searched all yesterday and then started today to look for her. There's a wine bottle over there."

"The forensic boys'll be along soon. I'll leave it for them. What on earth was she doing up here? Suicide? Took something with that wine?"

"Could be. She was obsessed with Jock Fleming, a painter who's visiting here. She told everyone she was engaged to him and flashed a diamond ring around. He denies the whole thing. She may have bought the ring herself. Mind you, there's a photo by her bedside signed, 'To my darling Effie. Jock.' "

They both began to search in wider circles around the body. "There's a plastic carrier bag over here with two glasses in it," called Hamish. "They look clean. Don't think anyone drank out of them."

They were sweating in the full heat of the sun. There is practically no pollution in the far north of Scotland, and the sun that day was fierce.

"You'd think it would be cooler this far up," complained Jimmy. "We'd better not mess up the scene. Let's sit over there where your girlfriend is and get a bit of shade."

They joined Priscilla. "Find anything?" she asked.

"No," said Jimmy. "We can't do anything until the experts arrive."

A helicopter hovered overhead, and a ladder descended. Dr. Brodie scrambled down it.

"Where's the pathologist?" asked Hamish.

"Coming along," said Dr. Brodie. "I'm to do the preliminary examination."

He turned Effie over. "We need a tent or something. The body's cooking in this sun. It's still damp underneath. She must have lain here since that awful rain. Maybe exposure. I can certify her dead, but that's it."

"No sign of poisoning?" asked Hamish. "There's a wine bottle there. And that missing finger: Has it been sawn off, or did some animal bite it off?"

74

"I would say it had been hacked off with a penknife. That's the finger she had the engagement ring on."

"If she was suicidal," said Jimmy, "then maybe she hacked it off herself."

"So where is it?" asked Hamish. "I suppose it would be all right to look in her coat pockets in case there's a suicide note."

"I can see the forensic boys suiting up down below," said Jimmy. "They're starting to get into the police helicopter. No climbing for them."

Hamish went back to the body. "I'll just take a peek." Flies were buzzing around it, and he flapped at them angrily.

Effie was wearing a waxed coat with zip pockets. Hamish gently opened one and felt inside. "Yuk!" he exclaimed. "The finger's in her coat pocket. No ring."

"Man, don't poke around any more," said Jimmy, "or Blair'll have your guts for garters."

Hamish searched in her other pocket. "There's a piece of folded paper here."

"Should you be opening that?" protested Dr. Brodie.

"I'm wearing gloves." Hamish unfolded the sheet of A-4 paper. It had been protected from the rain by the heavy waxed coat.

"I cannot live any more," he read. "I am going to lie out on the mountain until I die. Jock has killed me. Effie."

"Well, that solves that," called Jimmy. "She went daft and stayed out here until she died of exposure."

Hamish replaced the letter. "The letter's typewritten," he said. "She may not have written it."

"Come on, laddie. Don't go looking for murder when you've got a nice clean case of suicide. Oh, look what's dropping down from the heavens."

A helicopter hovered overhead, and down the ladder, cursing and sweating, came Detective Chief Inspector Blair.

He was followed, one by one, by the members of the forensic team. He ignored Hamish and said to Jimmy, "What have we got here?"

"Local artist, sir. Looks like suicide. There's a note in her pocket and in another pocket a finger — her ring finger. Looks like she hacked it off."

"You shouldnae ha' touched the body."

"I did that," said Hamish.

"I'll see to you later," snarled Blair. "Take yourself off and take that friend of yours with you. You can put in a report."

Priscilla and Hamish moved off down

the hill just as the forensic team were erecting a tent over the dead body.

"What do you think?" asked Priscilla.

"I think I want to get back to the police station, have a long cold drink, and think about this."

For once, when they got to where their cars were parked, Hamish was glad that Priscilla did not offer to join him. He wanted to be alone and think hard.

The first person he saw as he drove along the waterfront was Jock. There was no sign of his easel or paints. He was leaning against the wall staring moodily out over the loch.

Hamish stopped the Land Rover and got out. Jock turned and glanced at him and then turned back to the loch. "They've found her?" he asked.

"I'm afraid so. She's dead."

"How?"

"Maybe exposure. Have you any idea what she was doing up there?"

Jock turned back to face him. "That maybe was me. I went up to see her as soon as I got back. She tried to insist I had proposed marriage to her. I told her I had said no such thing. I then asked how the hell she thought she'd got pregnant. She began to cry, but after a bit she apologised and we talked a bit about painting. I said I'd heard about that place called Geordie's Cleft and that you could get a panoramic view of the area from there. I said I might climb up and have a look. She asked me why it was called Geordie's Cleft, and I told her the story. I was right sorry for the wee woman at the end. I told her we could be friends and left it at that."

"She had a photo of you beside her bed," said Hamish. "It was signed, 'To my darling Effie. Jock.' "

"Then she signed it herself. Leave me alone, Hamish. I'm feeling right bad about this."

Hamish went back to the police station, where the cat and dog stared at him balefully. "I know," said Hamish. "But it isnae my fault you've been on your own all day. Off you go. Take yourselves for a walk, and I'll have dinner ready for you when you get back."

They both slid out the door.

Hamish drank a large glass of water, went into the office, typed up his report, and sent it over. Then he went to Patel's and bought a bottle of whisky in the hope that Jimmy would call on him.

As if smelling the food he had cooked for

them, the dog and cat appeared back in the kitchen just as he was filling their bowls.

Hamish did not feel like eating. He kept turning facts over and over in his mind. He poured himself a small measure of whisky, added water, and went into his living room and sat down in an armchair.

He started and nearly spilled his drink when Sonsie jumped on his lap. "You're too heavy," he grumbled. The cat stared at him with yellow eyes. Lugs tried to struggle up as well but then contented himself by lying on the floor with his chin on Hamish's crossed ankles.

Hamish felt his eyes beginning to close. He set the glass down on the floor beside him. Soon he was asleep.

He awoke an hour later, roused by the hissing of the cat on his lap and the sound of someone calling, "Hamish!"

He saw Jimmy standing nervously in the doorway. "Call off that weird cat, Hamish," said Jimmy. "It looks ready to spring."

Hamish patted the cat and said, "Down you go. It's all right. It's only Jimmy. Let's go into the kitchen."

"I need a dram," said Jimmy, sitting down at the kitchen table. "That cat's scary. I'm telling you, I'm surprised you've got a hen left in the coop."

79

"Never mind the cat. What's the verdict?"

"Seems like suicide. Professor Jane Forsythe, the pathologist, says she can't be sure until she does an autopsy."

"That note was typewritten," said Hamish. "Anyone could have done it. And where's the knife?"

"What knife?"

"The one used to saw the finger off. Was it anywhere around or in another pocket? And where's the ring?"

"No, and no ring, and are you going to pour me a dram or keep it all to yourself?"

"Help yourself. The bottle's on the table."

"Look," said Jimmy, "if by any chance it was murder, who would want to kill her?"

"I don't know. Jock's ex-wife is in town. I might be having a word with her."

"Come on. Effie was mad. She was a fantasist."

"But was she an artist?"

"What do you mean?"

Hamish told him about the dust on the pottery wheel and the stiff, dirty brushes.

"Still, I don't see if that's got anything to do with it," said Jimmy.

"Unless she was ripping off some artist. Any news of the sister?"

"Yes, she's called Caro Garrard, and she's on her way up."

"We might find out something from her. Maybe it's someone from Effie's past."

"Who killed her? Come on, Hamish. It's suicide pure and simple."

Three more days crept past while Hamish fretted, trying to hear of any results. He had a good idea that Blair had blocked anyone from talking to him. At last, on the morning of the fourth day, he phoned Professor Jane Forsythe and reintroduced himself.

"Oh, the bright policeman from Lochdubh," she said. "How can I help you?"

"I wonder if you have completed the autopsy and found out how the woman died?"

"Effie Garrard died of a combination of ethylene glycol and exposure."

"What's ethylene glycol, and where can anyone get it?"

"Anywhere. It's commonly known as antifreeze."

"Wouldn't it taste awful?"

"No, it tastes sweet. Some alcoholics even drink it when they can't afford anything else. It was in that bottle of dessert wine that was found at the site."

"Any fingerprints on the bottle?"

81

"No. I mean, just those of the deceased."

"What about that sawn-off finger?"

"I can only assume she did it herself."

"With what? Nothing was found in the way of a knife or razor."

"She may have thrown it away. The procurator fiscal has decided on a verdict of suicide."

"I'm not sure about that."

"Well, your superiors are. Case closed. They say she was so mad and so disappointed in love that she killed herself."

"What are the symptoms of antifreeze poisoning?"

"It's changed in the body by the enzyme alcohol dehydrogenase into glycolic acid and oxalic acid, which are highly toxic compounds. There was widespread tissue injury to the brain, kidneys, liver, and blood vessels. After taking it, she would start to feel tired, disoriented, and may have fallen asleep."

Hamish thanked her, put the receiver down, and stared into space. It was all so neat and tidy, and yet he had an uneasy feeling about the whole thing. He wondered if Jock's wife was still in Lochdubh.

Cursing himself for not having tried to speak to her before, he hurried along to Sea View. Mrs. Dunne told him that Mrs.

Fleming had gone out for a walk.

"Do you know which direction she took?" asked Hamish.

"I saw her go in the direction of the bridge."

"When did she leave?"

"Just a few minutes ago."

Hamish set off in pursuit.

He saw a small blonde woman heading up the road on the other side of the humpback bridge.

He ran after her. "Mrs. Fleming?" he called.

She stopped and turned round. She was in her late thirties with dyed-blonde hair in a ponytail. She had small, discontented features and pale blue eyes. She was wearing a multicoloured blouse, brief khaki shorts, and sturdy boots.

"Yes?"

"Police Constable Hamish Macbeth, Mrs. Fleming. May I talk to you for a moment?"

"Go ahead, copper. But if it's aboot that dead wumman, I cannae help ye." Her voice was harsh with a Glaswegian accent.

"Did you know her?"

"Never heard o' her till I come here."

"Why did you and Jock divorce?"

"Away wi' ye, ye nosy copper. That's ma business."

She stared at him defiantly, her thin arms folded across her chest. "I've got naethin' mair to say to ye."

"Well, if you think of anything . . ."

She continued to stare at him defiantly until he walked away.

Hamish went back to the station and put on his climbing boots. He was determined to go up to Geordie's Cleft and look around.

First he phoned Angela and asked her if she would look after the dog and cat.

"Can't," she said. "Lugs is all right, but that wild cat of yours terrifies my cats. You'll need to find someone else."

In desperation, Hamish phoned Priscilla and explained his problem. "I'll come with you," she said in her calm, even voice. "There are no police around any more. We can take your Land Rover, put the animals in the back. I'll bring some food, and we'll drive up as far as we can. We can let them out for a run and then shut them up in the Land Rover while we climb up to Geordie's Cleft."

Hamish said he would pick her up. As he drove to the hotel, he couldn't help hoping that Betty had returned. He was still puzzled as to why she had left without phoning him.

Priscilla was waiting for him in the forecourt with a large picnic hamper.

"You were quick getting the food ready," said Hamish.

"A family had ordered it and then decided they didn't want it. They're being charged for it anyway, so it's free food for all of us."

Hamish drove as near Geordie's Cleft as he could, the Land Rover bumping over the heather. He stopped, and they got out. Lugs and Sonsie ran off together.

"They won't get lost, will they?" asked Priscilla anxiously.

"No, they always come back when I call. Anyway, if we eat before we climb, they'll smell the food and come running."

"I hadn't time to get animal food for them."

"They're spoilt. They're used to people food."

Sure enough, Priscilla was just lifting a whole roast chicken out of its container when Sonsie came loping up, followed by Lugs, the dog's odd, large ears flapping as he tried to keep up with the cat.

Hamish watched Priscilla as she deftly carved the chicken and separated the pieces out onto paper plates. The sun was shining down on the golden bell of her hair. What did she think? wondered Hamish. What did she think of him? Did she ever think of their broken engagement?

"I don't think your animals will like potato salad," said Priscilla. She gave each animal a plate of chicken pieces. "There's a bottle of wine here, or would you prefer coffee?"

"Coffee. There's a long climb ahead, and I need all my wits about me."

"So why are you still interested? It's all around the village that the poor woman committed suicide."

"There's something wrong. The pathologist says she died of a combination of antifreeze and exposure."

"The antifreeze having been in the wine bottle?"

"Yes. But evidently antifreeze tastes sweet, and it was a dessert wine."

"What are you getting at?"

"Just suppose someone really believes she's pregnant and that she's going to marry Jock. Jock calls on her and tells her he never meant to marry her and that she's talking rubbish. She's devastated. Yes, but what if she gets a message supposed to have come from Jock, saying something like, 'I'm sorry, Effie. I really do love you'? Say the message is left outside her door

86

with that bottle of wine. Say the message goes on asking her to bring the wine to Geordie's Cleft so they can toast their engagement. 'If I'm late, help yourself to a glass before I arrive.' "

"But how would she even know where Geordie's Cleft was?"

"Jock had told her he planned to go up there painting to get a panoramic view. He maybe told other people. So she sets off and climbs up and waits and waits. Decides to have a glass."

"Find the corkscrew?"

"Damn. That's another thing I've got to look for. So she feels disoriented and drowsy, maybe falls asleep. The killer's been waiting nearby. She pops that typewritten suicide note into Effie's pocket."

"She?"

"The ring finger, cut off. Could be a jealous rage."

"Or some man from her past."

"Could be." Hamish stood up. "I won't eat any more at the moment. The food's making me feel lazy. I'll shut up the animals, and we'll be on our way."

They set out on the long climb. The air was full of the scents of bell heather and thyme. Down below them lay the fishing village of Lochdubh with its neat rows of whitewashed Georgian houses.

A yacht cut a white trail through the calm blue waters of the loch. Smoke rose straight up from chimneys; a lot of the villagers, like Hamish, used the old-fashioned method of heating water.

Hamish suddenly wanted it to be suicide so they could all go on with their safe lives far from the murder, drugs, and mayhem of the cities.

"I'm beginning to dread newcomers," he said as they approached the cleft.

"There may be more in the future."

"Why?"

"With the European Union savagely cutting fishing quotas, a lot of the fishermen are thinking of turning their boats into tourist pleasure craft."

"I'm beginning to think no one in the village tells me anything any more," said Hamish. "First I've heard of it. I wonder what else they haven't been telling me."

They walked up to the cleft, then split up and began to search around. Although it was mostly rocky, there were a few stunted gorse bushes.

After an hour, Hamish said, "Nothing here. Let's try further afield. Now, if someone threw something, where would it land?"

"Maybe right down the slope and into those gorse bushes. Mind you, they're pretty far below."

They slithered down. Hamish lost his footing and went straight into the gorse bushes. "Ouch," he yelled. "Help me out of here. I'm all prickles."

Priscilla took his hand and helped him out. Hamish plucked gorse prickles out of his hair and his clothes.

"There's something glinting down in there," said Priscilla, peering into the shade of the bushes.

"Let me try," said Hamish. "A few more prickles won't matter."

She pointed. He pulled out a pair of latex gloves, bent down, and eased a long arm into the bushes. "Got it."

"What is it?"

"It's a corkscrew."

"That solves one problem."

"It's brand new."

"Maybe she bought it for the occasion."

"I wonder why the forensic boys didn't find it," said Hamish. "Mind you, that lot are more interested in drinking and rugby than in finding anything. The lot of them turn up on jobs with hangovers. Unless it was put there afterwards."

"I doubt it," said Priscilla. "No one

would want to be seen near the scene."

They searched further without finding anything else.

"I'd like a look at Effie's cottage," said Hamish. "Just to see if she had a corkscrew."

"Won't it be locked up?"

"There are ways of getting in. Come on."

CHAPTER FIVE

I've taken my fun where I've found it,
An' now I must pay for my fun,
For the more you have known o' the
others
The less you will settle for one;
An' the end of it's sittin' and thinkin',
An' dreamin' Hell-fires to see.
So be warned by my lot (which I know
you will not),
An' learn about women from me!
— Rudyard Kipling

Effie's cottage turned out to be locked. "It's just a simple Yale lock," said Hamish. He took out a thin piece of steel from one of his many pockets and popped the lock.

"What if the sister's here?" hissed Priscilla.

"I don't think she's come to Lochdubh yet. Probably making arrangements for the burial."

Hamish started to look through the

kitchen drawers. "Here we are!" he said triumphantly. "Not one but two cork-screws."

"So maybe she had three," said Priscilla. "I think we should go."

They walked outside, pulling the door behind them so that the lock clicked.

"Any sign of Betty Barnard coming back?" asked Hamish.

"I think she's due back tomorrow."

Hamish visibly brightened. Why could he not leave things alone and accept the procurator fiscal's verdict of suicide? Then perhaps he could have a few more days spent in Betty's company, driving around the Highlands.

"I think," he said, "that I'm being over-zealous. Maybe I'd chust better get on with things."

Priscilla eyed Hamish narrowly. She knew that his accent became more sibilant when he was angry or excited about something.

Hamish dropped Priscilla back at the hotel. Then he drove to the police station. He had not checked the morning's mail. He threw the usual junk into the trash bin and then found one from the bank in Braikie. He opened it up. There was a letter from the manager congratulating him on his bravery and a reward cheque for ten thousand pounds. Hamish stared at it in delight. He would send half the money to his family in Rogart. And with the other half? He had a holiday coming up. He could travel! He could go to New York and visit his cousin in Brooklyn.

To hell with Effie. It had surely been suicide.

There was a tentative knock at the front door. Hamish frowned. The locals always came to the kitchen door. He went through to the front and wrenched the little-used door open.

He stifled a gasp of surprise. A thick sea mist had rolled in, and for one moment, he thought he was looking at the ghost of Effie Garrard. Then the figure addressed him in an all-too-human voice: "Police Constable Macbeth? I am Caro Garrard, Effie's sister."

"Come ben," said Hamish. "We'll go into the kitchen. I've got the stove on. The mist makes things awfy cold and damp."

He shut the door behind her and then led the way to the kitchen. Lugs and Sonsie, who had been well fed, both raised their heads and stared at her and then went back to sleep.

"Sit down," said Hamish. "How can I help you?"

"I don't believe my sister committed suicide. The pathologist said to me that if I had any doubts about her death, perhaps I should talk to you. The police in Strathbane won't listen to me."

Hamish sat down opposite her. He could feel his dreams of visiting New York disappearing.

"What makes you think that?"

"I did not know Effie had been passing my work off as her own. She had a nervous breakdown last year over some man. She's always wanted to live in the Highlands. We were brought up in Oban. I said I would help her buy a little place. She then said she could sell some of my work and take a small commission to keep her going. I agreed. Things seemed to be going very well, and then she phoned me to say she was going to marry some artist called Jock Fleming.

"I was a bit nervous because before her breakdown, she had been up in court accused of stalking some businessman in Brighton. But she sounded so happy and confident. Then she phoned me to say he had jilted her. She was crying hard. I said I would get up to see her as soon as I could.

"But then she phoned me later that night. She sounded elated. She said that she had found a bottle of wine outside her door with a note from Jock asking her to meet him up at Geordie's Cleft. He said he really loved her.

"I tried to tell her that someone was playing a nasty trick on her. A man doesn't jilt a woman and then a few hours later tell her he loves her. But she wouldn't listen."

"Did you tell the police at headquarters about this?"

"They said Effie was mad. All she did was lie. They said her brain had turned and she went up there to commit suicide."

"Have you spoken to Jock Fleming?"

"Yes, earlier today. He was very distressed. He said he'd never proposed marriage to her. He said that she was chasing after him. Remembering Effie's behaviour in Brighton, I felt I had to believe him."

She clasped her hands in front of her. "I'm going to stay at Effie's cottage for a bit. Can you help me?"

O lost New York, swirling away in a grey mist like the mist outside, to be gone forever. Then Hamish brightened. Of course, all he had to do was delay his holiday leave.

"I'll do what I can," he said. "But I'm

95

short of suspects. Jock's ex-wife is here. I'll get to know her a bit better."

In the kitchen light, he noticed differences between Caro and her sister. Caro's hair was styled in a smooth bob, and she was wearing light make-up.

"Are you really sure," Hamish went on, "that you did not know that your sister was passing off your work as her own?"

"She wouldn't do that!"

"I assure you she did."

"I would have been really furious with her if I had known that. I haven't been to the cottage yet. The police gave me the keys. I really thought she might have started painting a bit on her own. Hal Addenfest told me she had some stuff in the hotel gift shop."

"Who is Hal Addenfest?"

"Some American tourist. I believe he took Effie out for a meal a couple of times."

Hamish began to wonder seriously why no one in the village was gossiping to him any more.

He told Caro he would keep in touch with her. After she had left, he phoned Priscilla. "What's this about some American called Hal Addenfest dating Effie?"

"Oh, him. The locals call him the Ugly

American. He's like an old-fashioned stereotype, bragging and thinking anyone outside the States is determined to cheat him."

"Priscilla, I didn't know until today of his existence. Why is no one telling me anything any more?"

"It started one day when Angela was wearing a brief pair of shorts. The Currie sisters called on you to tell you that you should do something about it. You told them you were sick of gossip and sent them off. They told everyone in the village not to gossip to you because it was making you furious."

"I've just seen Effie's sister. She said Effie phoned her the night she was murdered saying she had a note from Jock asking her to meet him at Geordie's Cleft. It was left with that bottle of wine."

"So why aren't the police all over the place investigating a murder?"

"Because they — probably Blair — insist that Effie was mad and never told the truth. I'll need to investigate it on my own. I'll be up at the hotel tomorrow."

Hal Addenfest went out for his usual constitutional walk the following morning, taking in great lungfuls of clear air. He was a retired businessman who had been chairman of a company. Because of the power of his situation, he had never known just how unpopular he was. When he retired, his wife left him, declaring she couldn't stand having him around all day.

He had fought the divorce case savagely, hiring the best lawyers, so that his wife ended up with very little. He was a little man, just under five feet tall, with a leathery face and small, suspicious eyes. But deep down in him was a romantic streak. *An American in Paris* had been one of the favourite films of his youth. So he had first relocated to Paris. He found the French standoffish and cold, particularly when he frequently snarled at them, "We pulled your chestnuts out of the fire in World War II."

His other favourite film had been *Brigadoon.* He turned his calculating eyes to the Scottish Highlands.

He found the hotel beautiful and the food excellent, but the locals baffled him, quite unaware that he baffled them. The village was occasionally visited by American tourists, courteous and polite. Hal was a type they had not met before.

Two days after his arrival, he had said to the hotel manager, Mr. Johnson, "How do

I get to meet the highlanders?"

Surprised, the manager said, "They're all around you."

"But," Hal protested, "where is this famous highland hospitality? They should be inviting me into their cottages for whisky and those things — bannocks."

"You'll need to make friends here, just as you made friends in the States," Mr. Johnson said.

But Hal had not made friends in the States. All his life he had been too busy clawing his small way up the corporate ladder. Once on top, he had been surrounded by enough sycophants to give him an illusion of popularity.

He was returning to the hotel when he noticed the tall figure of a policeman standing outside.

He went to walk past but found himself being hailed.

"Mr. Addenfest?"

"Yes?"

"I am Police Constable Hamish Macbeth. I'd like a wee word with you."

"What about?"

"Effie Garrard. Do you mind if we go inside?"

They went into the hotel lounge. "So what do you want to know?" demanded Hal.

"I believe you took her out a couple of times."

"So?"

They were interrupted by a maid placing a tray with coffee and biscuits in front of them.

"What's this?" demanded Hal angrily. "I didn't order anything."

"It's on the house," said the maid. "Mr. Johnson knows Hamish likes his coffee."

"I hope she doesn't expect a tip," grumbled Hal when the maid went off and stood by the door. "Yeah, Effie Garrard. I saw her stuff in the gift shop. It's good. I met her there, and we got talking. I took her out a couple of times. Expensive restaurants. Cost me nearly . . . Wait a bit." He took a small leather-bound notebook from his jacket pocket.

"Never mind," interrupted Hamish. "I want to know about Effie herself. Coffee?"

"Sure they aren't going to charge me for it?"

"*No!*"

"Keep your shirt on. Yes, Effie. Well, she was good company. She's had a very colourful life. She and her sister were brought up in an orphanage in Perth. Caro was adopted first, but they didn't want Effie. She was finally adopted by a family in Inverness. She said the woman beat her and the husband sexually abused her."

"What was the name of the people who adopted Effie?"

He took out his notebook again.

"Man, ye surely didn't sit taking notes while she was talking!" exclaimed Hamish.

"Afterwards. I'm going to write a book."

"We had an author over at Cnothan," said Hamish. "Someone murdered him."

"Here we are!" said Hal, ignoring Hamish's last remark. "Cullen, that was the name. George and Martha Cullen."

"And where in Inverness did they live?"

"Somewhere out on the Bewley Road."

"Did she give you the name of the orphanage?"

"Sorry."

"So what else did she say?"

"If what I tell you leads to the capture of someone, will I get a reward?"

"No."

Hal closed the notebook again. "Well, that's all, folks. You are wasting my valuable time. I've nothing more to say to you."

"What if I arrest you for impeding a police investigation?"

Hal grinned. "And what if I tell you what I know? The police have decided it's suicide. Case closed. So unless I hear differently, I'll keep any information about Effie I have to myself. You wanna know any more? Tell your bosses to phone me."

Hal got to his feet and, picking up the plate of biscuits, headed off for the stairs.

Priscilla came and sat down opposite Hamish. "How did you get on?"

"Horrible wee man."

"He's a one-off. We've got an American family staying here, and they run when they see him."

Hamish eyed her speculatively. "Hal wrote down everything Effie told him in a notebook. She told him she was brought up in an orphanage in Perth and subsequently adopted by a couple in Inverness who abused her. You couldn't charm some more information out of him?"

"I'll think about it."

Hamish returned to the police station. He found a George Cullen at an address in Sutherland Terrace which he remembered being off the Bewley Road. He phoned. When a man answered, Hamish introduced himself and asked, "Mr. George Cullen?"

"Aye, that's me."

"Did you adopt an Effie Garrard a long time ago?"

102

"We fostered her for a bit."

"May I come and talk to you?"

"Aye, any time. I'm long retired. Sad thing about her death."

"I'll leave now," said Hamish, "and be with you in just under an hour."

The Cullens' house was a small, granite Victorian villa. Hamish rang the bell, and an old stooped man answered the door.

"Mr. Cullen?"

"That's me. Come ben."

The living room into which Mr. Cullen ushered Hamish was dark and cold and strangely barren. No pictures, photographs, or books. A square table with upright chairs stood by the window. There was an armchair next to the two-bar electric fire. The carpet was old and faded.

"Sit down," said Mr. Cullen, indicating a chair at the table. He saw Hamish looking around and said, "The wife died last year. I got rid of nearly everything. All those things did were to remind me of her, and I was tired of grieving. How can I help you?"

"You fostered Effie Garrard?"

"Yes, that's right. She was twelve at the time. We couldn't cope. We had to get rid of her after a year."

"Why was that?"

"She was a congenital liar. She walked

103

into a police station and said my wife was beating her and I was sexually abusing her. Oh, the scandal. Thank God it didn't get into the papers. The police medical examiner found she was still a virgin and hadn't a mark on her. We couldn't bear to have her in the house after that."

"Do you know where she went?"

"No, and I didn't want to know."

"What was the name of the orphanage you got her from?"

"It wasn't an orphanage. We got her through the social services."

"Did you think Effie had mental troubles?"

"To be frank, I'm surprised she killed herself. I always thought *she* would kill someone."

"Why?"

"At the beginning, my wife doted on Effie. She wasn't a pretty child, but seemed cute and clever. Then my wife began to get vomiting attacks. One day I thought I saw Effie put something in my wife's tea. I told her and said she wasn't to eat or drink anything that Effie had been near. She protested but did as I said, and the attacks stopped. Then there was the sexual abuse business. That was enough."

"What about her real parents?"

"I remember being told the mother was dead and the father was an abusive drunk, which is why the girls had been taken away from him."

Hamish thanked him and left. He decided it would be a good idea to visit Caro, but when he arrived at the police station, it was to find Archie Macleod, the fisherman, waiting for him.

"What brings you?" asked Hamish. "Just a chat?"

"No. Now, I know it's been going around that you don't like gossip . . ."

"I've just learned the Currie sisters have been warning everyone off. For heaven's sake, tell everyone I'm interested in every bit of gossip. I couldnae do my job otherwise. Come in and sit down and tell me what you know."

Archie went into the kitchen, patted Lugs, eyed Sonsie warily, and sat down. "I heard tell you're interested in a wee bit o' gossip now. It's like this. Henry, the gamekeeper, was up on the hill the evening Effie we suppose disappeared. He had his binoculars to his eyes, scanning for poachers. He saw Jock going into Effie's cottage. A few minutes later, he came out. You know how sound carries up on the moors. He couldn't hear the words, but Jock was shouting and he looked to be in a right rage.

"Then half an hour later, that wee blonde woman that was married to Jock turned up. Henry was curious because we all knew about Effie making up all that stuff about her engagement and pregnancy. Mrs. Fleming wasn't allowed in, but she stood on the doorstep until Effie slammed the door in her face. Henry was real interested in the show, so he kept his glasses on the cottage. He was just losing interest when he saw another wee woman drive up. At first, he thought he was seeing things because she looked a good bit like Effie. Well, that woman didn't reappear after Effie let her in, so Henry got bored and went back to work."

"Thanks, Archie. I'd better see the sister and the ex-wife again. I mean, for one thing, the sister was supposed to have arrived *after* Effie's death. Surely it couldn't have been her. The police contacted her in Brighton."

After Archie had left, Hamish phoned Jimmy Anderson on his mobile. "Jimmy," said Hamish, "could you do me a favour and find out if the police contacted Caro Garrard, Effie's sister, or if she got in touch with them?"

"Trying to turn a suicide into a murder?"

"Just checking everything. Where are you?"

"Walking into police headquarters. I'll call you back."

After a quarter of an hour, Jimmy phoned. "Caro Garrard phoned the police at Strathbane and said she was Effie's sister. That was after the death appeared in the newspapers. She said she was in Brighton and would be travelling up."

Hamish thanked him and then walked out of the police station and along to the schoolhouse, where Matthew Campbell, the reporter, lived with his wife, Freda.

Matthew and Freda gave him a warm welcome. "It's a duty call," said Hamish. "Did the story about Effie Garrard's death get into the nationals?"

"No," said Matthew. "Well, there was a bit in the Glasgow editions, but nothing got south. Why?"

"Can't tell you at the moment, but I think I'm on to something."

"If it's a good story, don't keep me in the dark, Hamish."

"You'll be the first to know."

Hamish drove up to Effie's cottage, his brain in a turmoil. Jock had given the impression that he and Effie had parted amicably. And the sister, Caro? She could easily have phoned from somewhere near Lochdubh after visiting Effie and pretended she was still in Brighton. But if she were guilty of anything, why would she have pressed him to find out if her sister had been murdered?

She answered the door to him. The room looked more welcoming in the glow of several oil lamps than when he had last visited it.

Hamish was momentarily diverted. "Where did you get the lamps?" he asked. "I thought they were hard to come by now."

"I got them at an auction in Inverness. They didn't cost much."

"You were lucky. When electricity came to the Highlands, the Hydro Electric Board led people to believe that electricity was going to be cheap. So they got rid of all the old oil lamps, and now collectors are looking for them. Isn't the electricity working?"

"It's supplied here by a generator. I like the light from oil lamps."

She probably had antifreeze for the generator, thought Hamish. He removed his peaked cap, sat down at the table, and ran his long fingers through his fiery red hair.

"I have a problem," he said.

Caro sat down next to him. She was wearing a long Indian gown of crushed velvet decorated with little pieces of sparkling mirror. Her perfume smelled like sandalwood.

"What problem?"

"You were seen the evening afore Effie disappeared calling here at the cottage. Henry, the gamekeeper, was up on the hill scanning the area with a pair of binoculars looking for poachers, and he saw you arrive."

She bent her head. "I didn't like to tell you."

"Why? If you want me to find out whether your sister was killed or not, I need every bit of information I can get. Now, let's have the truth."

She gave a little sigh and then began to speak in a low voice. "I wanted to find out whether she had been murdered, but I feared that if you knew I had called on her that evening, it would look suspicious."

"Go on."

"My foster parents were good people. They died when I was twenty-eight. I had already graduated from Glasgow School of Art and moved down to Brighton."

Hamish's hazel eyes sharpened. "Did

109

you know Jock Fleming when you were at the college?"

She shook her head. "In Brighton, I began to build up a reputation for myself as an artist. *Vogue* did an article on Brighton, and I was featured in the magazine. Two days later, Effie turned up. I was delighted to see her. She said she had no money and nowhere to go, and so I said she could live with me. I was dating another artist and hoped to become engaged to him. He told me Effie was bothering him, phoning him up, trying to see him. I didn't want to believe him because I was so thrilled to have found my sister. Then one day he told me he had gone to the police to get an injunction taken out against her to stop her from stalking him. I confronted Effie, who burst into tears. She showed me letters from him, passionate love letters. I believed Effie. I refused to see the man again. The next thing I knew she was up in court for breaking the injunction. It all came out. She had forged the letters. I was going to throw her out, but she had a nervous breakdown.

"When she recovered, she was so contrite and so miserable. She said she'd always wanted to go back to Scotland, and I saw a way of getting her out of my hair. I was well-off. My foster parents had left me a great deal of money in their will. I saw a way of still caring for Effie but getting her out of Brighton. I told her if she found a cheap place in Scotland, I would buy it for her. So she found this cottage, and I paid. Then she said she could sell some of my small paintings and pottery. I agreed because I thought it would give her something to do.

"I was having an exhibition in Brighton. A visitor said he had seen similar work to mine in the Highlands but by Effie Garrard, not Caro. I pressed him for details, and that is how I found that Effie had been passing my work off as her own. As soon as the exhibition was over, I drove up here."

Hamish interrupted her. "But you told me twice that you did not know Effie was pretending that your work was hers!"

"I lied. There was still something in me that wanted to protect her. I told her I was having nothing more to do with her, that she was on her own. She began to cry. But I was determined this time to get rid of her. I said I would come in the morning and pick up my stuff and then collect the rest from wherever she had tried to sell it.

"Then I opened the door to leave. There was a bottle of wine on the step with a note

111

attached to it. I yelled, 'Message for you,' and went to my car. She ran out of the house and read the note and then ran up to the car and hammered on the window. She said I could go to hell because some local artist, Jock Fleming, was in love with her and they were going to be married. She was elated, triumphant.

"I said, 'I don't know how you did it, Effie, but you probably wrote that note yourself. You're mad.' And then I drove off."

"What did you do then?" asked Hamish.

"I felt sickened. I decided to motor down to Glasgow and see a few old friends and then come back up when I was feeling calmer. Then I read about her death. I immediately thought someone had murdered her. I didn't want the police to know I'd been there. I panicked. I phoned them and said I was coming up from Brighton. I used my mobile phone. And that's it. Everything I'd come to know about Effie made me think of murder. Then I learned about Jock Fleming and about how she had been lying about an engagement, a pregnancy, and how she had even gone as far as buying an engagement ring. I couldn't suspect Jock because to me it was the Brighton business all over again. I went to see Jock just to be sure and showed him a signed photograph of him she'd had on her bedside table. He said the writing was a forgery and showed me samples of his own handwriting to prove it."

She fell silent.

Hamish said, "But you must be glad she's dead."

"In a way, yes, there's relief there. But I don't want to think there's a murderer out there thinking he's got away with it. Will you have to report what I've said?"

"No, as far as the police are concerned, it's suicide, and they don't want to think about any other solution. I'll keep in touch with you. Was Effie always a bit weird?"

"No, at one time she seemed pretty normal — or as normal as we both could be with that father of ours. He would get drunk and beat us. He sexually abused me and had Effie watch. Effie went numb and quiet. I couldn't bear it any longer. I was twelve years old, and Effie was eleven. I walked into the police station in Oban and told them. They had me examined and found I was telling the truth. Effie and I were taken into care by the social services. They tried to find us a home together, but we had to be split up. I never saw her again until she walked into that gallery in

Brighton. I was so sorry for her, remembering the abuse we had suffered." Caro began to cry. "What a mess."

Hamish went over to the kitchen area, where he found a bottle of whisky. He poured her a shot and took it back to her. "Drink that down," he said.

She took a gulp of whisky and dried her eyes with a corner of her dress. Hamish took out a clean handkerchief and handed it to her. "Use this," he said. "You'll cut your eyes on those wee bits o' glass on your frock."

Caro gave him a weak smile.

"Did Effie say anything to you about an American who had been taking her out?" asked Hamish.

"Not a word. Who is he?"

"Some chap who lives up at the hotel. He only took her out a couple of times. I'd better be on my way. I've got someone else to see."

Hamish drove down to the Sea View boarding house and asked Mrs. Dunne if Mrs. Fleming was in.

"She is that," said Mrs. Dunne, "but she's up in her room, and no gentlemen are allowed to visit ladies in their rooms. This is a respectable house."

"Chust tell her I'm here," said Hamish crossly, "and ask her to come down."

Mrs. Fleming came into the lounge, looking tired and sulky. "Whit now?" she demanded.

Hamish took out his notebook. "Sit down," he commanded. "Full name."

"Dora Fleming. Whit . . . ?"

"Maiden name."

"Harris."

Hamish sat down opposite her. "Where are your children?"

"With ma mither."

"And what brought you to Lochdubh?"

"I thocht it was time Jock was paying a bit mair."

"Right, now let's get to it. On the evening Effie Garrard disappeared, you were seen calling at her cottage."

"I never did!"

"Don't lie. You were seen. What did you talk about?"

She picked nervously at her nail varnish. "I telt her to stop bothering Jock. I told her she was right daft, making up all them stories."

"And what did she say to that?"

"She hadn't let me in. She slammed the door in my face."

The extreme Glasgow accent was leaving her voice. Did she speak in a coarse voice

115

because of a sort of inverted snobbery? wondered Hamish.

"And that was all that happened?"

"Swear to God."

"So why did you say nothing of this to the police?"

"I was feart they would suspect me. I thought it was murder at first, see, but when I heard it was the suicide, it was too late and the police werenae interested anyway."

"If you can think of anything else, let me know," said Hamish.

"So she was murdered?"

"Just making enquiries."

Now for Jock, thought Hamish.

CHAPTER SIX

*He had by nature a tarnishing eye that
cast discolouration.*
— George Meredith

Bessie Jamieson, the maid at the hotel who
had served Hal and Hamish coffee, had
stood a little way away from them, listening
to every word. She told the hotel porter,
Sammy, that Hamish had been trying to
find out what Hal had written in his notebook. Sammy told his mother that Hal was
some sort of government spy and he was
taking notes of what everyone said or did.
The gossip flew around Lochdubh.

"Disgraceful," said Nessie Currie to
Mrs. Wellington. "He should be stopped."

"You can't stop a man taking notes,"
said Mrs. Wellington. "There's probably an
innocent explanation. Ask Hamish Macbeth."

But Hamish was not at the police station.
He had asked to see Jock at Sea View after
he had finished interviewing Dora Fleming,

but was told by Mrs. Dunne that Jock had moved to the Tommel Castle Hotel, where he was painting a portrait of Miss Halburton-Smythe.

Hamish had a sudden jealous wish that Jock would turn out to be a murderer. At the hotel, he was told by the manager that Jock had been given an empty room at the top of the hotel as a temporary studio.

He rapidly mounted the stairs. A lift had not yet been installed in the hotel, although one was scheduled. He had an awful dread that he would find Priscilla posing naked.

But when he opened the door, it was to find the room deserted. An easel was set up with a cloth over it.

He peered under the cloth. There was a preliminary sketch of Priscilla with all her clothes on.

Hamish ran down the stairs again to find Jock walking into the hotel.

"A word with you," said Hamish grimly.

"All right," said Jock amiably. They walked into the lounge.

Bessie, the maid, saw them and ran to the kitchen to get coffee and biscuits to serve to them in the hope of hearing some more gossip.

"You were seen at Effie's cottage the evening she disappeared," began Hamish.

118

"I told you that."

"What you didn't tell me was that you had a shouting, screaming row."

"Who told you that?"

"Never mind."

"You know," said Jock, "in the city, no one ever knows what you're doing, but up here you can be walking across deserted moorland with not a soul in sight and in the evening someone will say they saw you and did you have a good walk?"

"So what really happened?"

Bessie hurried in with a tray of coffee and biscuits and set it on the table in front of them. She retreated to a corner of the lounge and stood expectantly.

"That'll be all, Bessie," said Hamish. "Thank you for the coffee. We'll ring if we need you."

Bessie reluctantly went out. Hamish rose and closed the door behind her, then came back to join Jock.

"When I thought it might be murder," said Jock, "I knew it would look bad for me if I'd said we had a blazing row. Truth is she gave me a fair scunner, begging and pleading and trying to kiss me. Truth is I shouted at her that if she came near me again, I would kill her. I said she was mad. But I didn't kill her."

"I'll tell you this," said Hamish, "but keep it to yourself for the moment. Later that evening, someone left a note for her with a bottle of wine supposed to have come from you and asking her to meet you at Geordie's Cleft. Now, if you were so harsh with her, and mad as she was, what on earth would make her think you would want to see her?"

Jock hung his head.

"Come on, man," snapped Hamish. "Out with it!"

"When I got back," said Jock, "I began to feel right sorry for her. I admired her work. Good artists are rare, and we're all a bit mad. So I phoned her. She'd given me her mobile number a while ago. I thought she needed help, therapy of some sort. I told her I was sorry I had been harsh and we'd meet to talk things over. I said I wouldn't be around the following day because I planned to go up to Geordie's Cleft."

"And what did she say?"

"Her phone was switched off, so I left a message."

"So that's why she believed the note."

"Is there any hope it might have been suicide?"

"I really don't think so," said Hamish.

"I mean, maybe when I didn't turn up, she decided to take her own life."

"That would mean she would need to have carried antifreeze up the mountain with her. The antifreeze was in the wine bottle. There must have been something in that note to tell her to go ahead and take a drink before you arrived. She would have one and, as time dragged on, maybe another. Why did you and Dora get divorced?"

"The usual story. Married in a rush and then found out it was a mistake. But when the kids came along, I tried to stick it out. But things got worse and worse. Dora would never leave me alone when I was working. If I had an exhibition, she'd turn up and make a scene. I found out she had been having an affair behind my back. I said if she didn't settle for an amicable divorce, it would all come out in court and the children would be taken away from her."

"So what's she doing up here? Money?"

"No, she likes haunting me. I don't know how she found out I was up here. Don't worry. She'll soon get tired of the game."

"You're painting a portrait of Miss Halburton-Smythe."

"Trying to. She's a beautiful woman."

121

Jock looked sharply at Hamish. "And that's all she is to me — a subject to paint."

Hamish eyed him cynically. "I thought you artists were always looking for interesting faces, craggy faces, things like that."

"Usually. But there's a remoteness about her which goes along with this landscape that I would like to capture. Oh, here's Betty."

Hamish brightened as Betty Barnard walked in. His official holiday was due the following week. He had planned to use the time trying to find out how Effie had been killed. He decided to cancel his holiday. That way he would not waste his leave, and he could maybe spend a few more pleasant days with Betty.

"Hullo, Jock, Hamish." She sat down. "No one drinking this coffee?" She poured herself a cup.

"Hamish is interrogating me," said Jock.

Her eyes flew to Hamish. "Why? What's happened?"

"The death of Effie Garrard."

"Oh, that. But that's a suicide."

"I think it might be murder," said Hamish.

"Why?"

"On the evening Effie went missing, someone left a bottle of wine with a note

122

supposed to be from Jock here asking Effie to meet him up at Geordie's Cleft."

"So why aren't there still police and detectives crawling all over the village?"

"Police headquarters have decided it was suicide and don't want to investigate any further."

"So why bother?"

"I don't like to think of a murderer loose in my village."

"That's a pity. I was hoping we could maybe spend the day together tomorrow. I was going to phone you."

Hamish thought quickly. "Maybe just an afternoon, if that's all right with you."

"Okay, I'll pick you up at one o'clock tomorrow. Now, if you've finished with Jock, leave us alone to discuss business."

Hamish drove down to the village and went into Patel's grocery store. He asked Mr. Patel, "Do you sell much antifreeze?"

"Don't stock it. Most folks go to Iain to get their cars serviced, and he supplies the antifreeze."

Iain Chisholm was working on the engine of an old Volvo in his garage. He straightened up when he saw Hamish.

"Do you ever sell antifreeze to anyone?" asked Hamish.

"No, there's no need. I put it in when I service their cars."

"Any missing?"

Iain pushed back his oily cap and stared around the dusty jumble of his garage. Then he went over to a row of shelves. "I've got two containers of the stuff here. I'm sure that's all I had."

"Could anyone have helped themselves while your back was turned?"

"I suppose they could. What's this about?"

"Effie Garrard. Herself died from drinking antifreeze. Who's been in here lately to get repairs or servicing?"

"The doctor, Mrs. Wellington, Mr. Johnson with two of the hotel cars, and that's about it."

"Do you ever leave the garage un-attended?"

"I lock it up. Not that there's thieves here, but the locals will nip in and take a spanner or something like that and forget to give it back. Hamish, if anyone wanted antifreeze, they've only got to stop at any garage out-side or inside Strathbane and buy some."

Hamish went to the police station to find Priscilla waiting for him in the kitchen. He kept a spare key in the gutter above the kitchen door.

"I've taken Sonsie and Lugs for a walk," said Priscilla. "They've been fed. Archie gave me some fish for Sonsie, and I bought some liver for Lugs."

"Did you find out anything more about the American?" asked Hamish.

"I invited him to join me for dinner. It was quite an ordeal. He kept taking out a notebook and scribbling in it under the table. It's all round the village he's a government spy."

"Who for? The CIA? How can people be so daft?"

"It made me furious. I told him if he didn't stop taking notes about what I was saying, then I'd put the dinner on his bill."

Hamish grinned. "I bet that stopped him in his tracks."

"He has ambitions to be an author."

"Good luck to him. I'd like to get a look at that notebook of his." Hamish looked hopefully at Priscilla.

"No hope, Hamish. I'll bet he sleeps with it under his pillow. Any leads?"

Hamish told her about his various interviews and then said, "I want to get to the bottom of this. Blair's behaved disgracefully in insisting it's a suicide. I could have done with a whole forensic team and policemen helping me to interview everyone."

"I'm afraid some members of the Strathbane forensic team are in trouble. I met Matthew on the road here, and he told me."

"What have they been up to now?"

"They'd just got a delivery of those blue light things, you know the ones that bring up bloodstains?"

"Yes."

"Well, they were using them to play *Star Wars* outside their favourite pub in Strathbane. They were all charged with drunk and disorderly and misuse of police property. They were even dressed up as *Star Wars* characters. I believe Luke Skywalker was particularly abusive."

Hamish groaned. "I'm beginning to think that lot are never sober. I'd better get on the phone and cancel my leave."

The following afternoon, Hamish spent a pleasant time with Betty. She listened to him as he felt no one had listened to him before. He began to wonder what it would be like to be married to an artists' agent. Then he wondered uneasily about Elspeth Grant, the reporter who was now back at her job in Glasgow. He had been thinking of proposing to her but had left it too late. He had tried calling her at various times, but she had hung up on him.

He was just leaving Betty at the hotel and about to get into the police Land Rover when Priscilla came running out. "Hamish! Hal's gone missing, and his bed hasn't been slept in."

"When did anyone last see him?"

"Yesterday. He took a packed lunch and said he was going for a walk. A lot of us have been out looking for him all day."

Hamish phoned Strathbane and alerted them that an American tourist had gone missing. Then he phoned the Mountain Rescue Patrol.

"I'll come into the hotel and find out if anyone saw him leave and which direction he went."

Mr. Johnson summoned the staff. When questioned, they all said they hadn't noticed where the American had gone. Then the maid, Bessie, came on duty and asked what all the fuss was about.

When Hamish told her, she said, "But he did come back!"

"When?"

"Last night. Just before dinner. I'd been taking a tray up to poor Mrs. Tabolt, who's feeling poorly. She's in the room next to him. I saw him going into his room."

"What time?"

"It would be about seven o'clock in the evening."

Hamish phoned the Mountain Rescue Patrol again and told them to hold off the search for the moment and then phoned Strathbane and said he was about to search Hal's room.

Mr. Johnson took him up to Hal's room. The door wasn't locked. Hamish went in. The bed was made up and obviously hadn't been slept in. Lots of clothes were in the wardrobe. Hamish searched every bit of the room, looking for Hal's notebook, but it was nowhere to be found.

"Let's check if his car is outside. He may have decided to drive somewhere," said Hamish.

But Hal's car was in the car park.

Hamish began to feel nervous. That wretched notebook, he thought. He phoned Strathbane once again and said he would need a team up to help him search. He knew they would turn out for a missing American tourist where they wouldn't budge for a local artist.

He went out into the moors around the hotel, calling and searching. At last, exhausted, he returned to the police station, having decided to start the search again in the morning. The nights were still light, and the weather was warm. There would be no danger of the wee man dying of exposure unless he had decided to climb up into the mountains.

Two local schoolboys, Sean and Diarmuid Hamilton, found the long white nights exciting. It was hard to sleep. They'd made an agreement earlier to slip out of their cottage and go down to the loch and play at chukkies — seeing how far they could skim a flat stone across the water.

In the grey gloaming which was like an early dawn just before the sun comes up, Diarmuid, proud possessor of a pencil torch, searched the shingly beach for flat stones. He swept the torch this way and that. The beam caught a pair of eyes down by the edge of the water.

"A seal, Sean," he called. "Come and look. Slowly, now. We don't want to frighten the beast."

They crept closer.

"Oh, hell," gasped Diarmuid. "It's a man!"

They turned and ran as hard as they could, scrambling up the steps to the waterfront and hurtling towards the police station.

Hamish was aroused from a deep sleep

by the sound of hammering on the door and the sharp barking of Lugs.

When he opened the door, he looked down into the ashen faces of two small boys.

"There's a deid man down by the loch," gasped Diarmuid.

"Come into the kitchen and sit down while I get myself dressed," said Hamish.

He went back into the bedroom and scrambled into his uniform. He hoped against hope the boys were mistaken and it would turn out to be nothing more than a bundle of old clothes.

When he was ready, he walked down with them to the beach, carrying a torch.

"Ower there," said Diarmuid, pointing.

In the peculiar grey light of a highland summer night, Hamish saw the body. He crouched down. The dead eyes of Hal Addenfest stared up at him. He was lying half in and half out of the water.

Hamish stood up and took out his mobile phone and called Strathbane. He turned to the boys. "Run along home. I'll be along to see you later."

The boys ran off. Hamish crouched down by the body again. He felt for a pulse and found none. He pulled on a pair of latex gloves and gently began to search in the pockets. Hal's wallet was there, with money and credit cards. But there was no sign of his notebook.

He gently turned the head to one side and felt the skull. It gave beneath his probing fingers. Someone had smashed Hal's skull in. The top half of the body, which was out of the water, was dry. There was no blood around the head that he could see. He looked at his watch. One in the morning. High tide had been two hours before, so allowing the time for the tide to recede, Hal must have been killed or placed on the beach a short time before the boys found him.

How could the killer have managed it unobserved? There were old people in Lochdubh who slept badly. Sound carried. Someone would surely have heard something.

He retreated to a flat rock and sat down. He took out his notebook and drew a plan of where the body was lying. Then on another page, he wrote down the boys' names and when they had called at the police station. A little breeze rippled the glassy surface of the loch, bringing with it the scent of pine from the forests on the other side.

At last, he could hear the distant wail of police sirens. They came ever nearer and ever louder. Lights started to go on in the cottages. The peace of the summer night was being ripped apart.

Police cars stopped on the waterfront. He could see the heavy figure of Blair approaching the steps. Blair slipped on a piece of seaweed and crashed down the steps and fell with a shriek of pain.

Hamish ran towards him. "I've broke my leg," howled Blair.

"Don't move," said Hamish, seeing the forensic team's white van coming along the waterfront. He called Dr. Brodie. Jimmy Anderson came down the steps to join him. "Tell the forensic boys to get a stretcher down here," ordered Hamish.

When Blair was carried up to the waterfront and was being examined by Dr. Brodie, who had come hurrying up with a coat over his pyjamas, Jimmy said, "So who's dead?"

"An American tourist called Hal Addenfest. He was staying at the Tommel Castle Hotel."

"That's the one you reported missing?"

"The same."

"Let's have a look." They walked down to where Hal was lying.

"He got a sore dunt in the back of his head," said Hamish.

132

"He might have fallen down the steps and dragged himself to the water's edge," said Jimmy. "Look at what's just happened to Blair."

Another siren sounded in the distance. "That'll probably be the ambulance from Braikie Hospital," said Hamish. "Blair must really have broken his leg."

When Blair was loaded into the ambulance, Jimmy and Hamish were joined by the pathologist, Professor Jane Forsythe. "He's got a crack on the back of his head," said Hamish.

She examined the body carefully and then straightened up. "I'll be able to tell you better what happened to him when I do the autopsy, but, yes, I would guess he had been killed by a blow to the head."

The forensic team started their work. A cameraman took pictures. A small crowd of villagers had gathered on the waterfront.

"His notebook's missing," said Hamish.

"What notebook?" asked Jimmy.

"He said he was going to be a writer. He took notes of what people said. He took Effie Garrard out a couple of times. I asked to see his notes about what she had said to him, but he refused. I couldn't press him because it wasn't a murder investigation."

"And you think it is now?"

"I think it always should ha' been. I'll be off and talk to the wee boys who found him, and then I'd better check if a rowing boat has been used. Someone could have taken him out in a boat, cracked him on the head, and left him on the beach."

"So why not just give him to the fishes?"

"I don't know. Maybe someone planned to take him off in a car and dump him somewhere where we wouldn't find him. I'll start in the morning and talk to all the people whose cottage windows overlook the loch."

"I'll have plenty of men to help you. Every damn cottage seems to overlook the loch."

"I suppose you're in charge of the case now, Jimmy."

"Aye. Great, isn't it?"

"I would suggest you start by reopening the case on Effie. I'll tell you everything I've got."

Jimmy sighed. "It's going to be a long night. I'll call on you in the morning. I want bacon, sausage, eggs, and whisky."

Hamish grinned and touched his cap. "Yes, sir!"

Hamish went to the Hamiltons' cottage. Their father said they had kept the boys up, knowing the police would want to talk to them.

Diarmuid and Sean were in the living room, drinking cocoa and being watched over by their anxious mother.

"Now, boys," said Hamish, "how soon after you left your home did you find the body?"

"About ten minutes," said Diarmuid. "We went out to throw stones in the loch. I thought it was a seal. Then I saw it was a deid man."

"Did you see or hear anything or anyone else?"

Their eyes widened with fright. "You mean the murderer might still ha' been around?" asked Sean.

"Maybe."

The boys looked at each other and then shook their heads. "It was awfy quiet," said Sean. "Not a sound."

"I'll take statements from you both later. Off to bed with you and try to get some sleep."

Mr. Hamilton let Hamish out. "They're good boys," he said.

"I know," said Hamish. "They didn't mean any harm. I doubt if they'll be sneaking out for some time to come."

As Hamish walked towards the police station, he saw police were already interviewing the villagers who had gathered. He decided to catch a few hours' sleep, relieved that Blair was not on the case or Hamish would have been allowed no sleep at all.

He set the alarm for six o'clock and climbed into bed, followed by his dog and cat. His last thought was that he should stop them from sleeping on his bed. What if his friendship with Betty progressed to something more?

The shrill sound of Hamish's alarm clock woke him. He struggled out of bed, feeling as if he had not slept at all. The dog and cat moved into the warm space in the bed left by his body and went back to sleep.

He washed and shaved, put on his uniform, and went out to the hen house to collect eggs for Jimmy's breakfast.

He went back in with the eggs in his cap, set them on the kitchen table, lit the stove, and was just putting the frying pan on it when a knock at the kitchen door heralded the arrival of Jimmy. The detective's foxy face looked tired, and his eyes were bloodshot.

"Give me a dram, Hamish. I'm fair worn out."

Hamish poured him some whisky and began to fry up breakfast. "So what's new?" he asked.

"Damn all," said Jimmy. "Nobody saw or heard anything. Forensic have moved their search to the rowing boats."

"I'm sure it's connected with Effie's murder."

"Still on about that? Why?"

"You may have learned from talking to the villagers that because of that notebook of his, they thought Hal was some sort of spy. But I don't think any of them are to blame. I think the murderer of Effie is still around and thought that Hal had something in that book that would be incriminating. I hadn't any help before, but now you can start digging into backgrounds. There's Effie's sister, Caro, the ex-wife, and Jock himself." He told Jimmy what the gamekeeper had seen.

"I learned Jock's agent is up here. What about her?"

"Not likely," said Hamish, blushing slightly as he set Jimmy's breakfast in front of him on the table.

"Oho!" said Jimmy. "Why the red face, Hamish? Fancy her, do you?"

"She's a perfectly nice woman," said Hamish defensively. Then he said, "What I was wondering was whether there was any madness in Caro, anything in her background — drugs, mental breakdown, anything. I think she'd had enough of Effie's shenanigans, and Effie passing off Caro's work as her own might have been the last straw.

"Then there's Jock Fleming. He has a blazing row with her and then phones her later, he says, to be kind."

Jimmy yawned. "When I've finished this, Hamish, I'll use your bed for a few hours' kip."

"Take the bed in the cell."

"Bound to be as hard as nails. Are you squeamish about me sleeping in your bed?"

"No, but the dog and cat are there, and they wouldnae take kindly to be disturbed."

"Hamish! They are not humans. They're animals. Get yourself a woman. Oh, stop glaring at me and put me in the cell."

"How's Blair?"

"In hospital. Not only a broken leg but a broken collarbone as well. He'll be out of commission for a while."

"Think they'll let you run the case, or will they bring in some horror from Glasgow or Inverness like they've done before?"

"I think I'm safe provided we get a quick result. You were due to go on holiday, weren't you? I hope you didn't book up anywhere, because your leave has been cancelled."

"I'd already cancelled it," said Hamish, opening the door of the one cell in the police station. "Pleasant dreams."

Hamish did a few chores around the police station and checked on his sheep before rousing the dog and cat.

"We're off to the Tommel Castle Hotel," he said. "You can have a run around while I'm interviewing folks."

He helped them up into the Land Rover and drove off. It was wonderful not to have Blair rampaging around.

At the hotel, he let Sonsie and Lugs out and made his way round to the back door and walked into the kitchen.

Clarry, the chef, was supervising his assistants, who were getting the hotel breakfasts ready.

"Have you time for a chat?" asked Hamish.

"Yes, we've only a few early birds. The rush doesn't start until nine o'clock."

In the days when Hamish had been made a sergeant and before his subsequent demotion, Clarry had been his policeman. But it had turned out that Clarry's only interest was in cooking, and he had subsequently retired from the force to work at the hotel.

Hamish sat down next to Clarry. "You've heard about the death of Mr. Addenfest?"

"Yes, first thing I heard when I came on duty."

"Did you speak to him yesterday?"

"I had words with him."

"What about?"

"He'd ordered a packed lunch earlier. He came into the kitchen in the early evening to complain that what he was being charged for the packed lunches was much more than the contents were worth. I told him we supplied the best packed lunches in Scotland and if he had any complaints, he could take them to the manager. He asked me my name and wrote it down in that notebook he was always carrying around. He said, 'I'm wise to the lot of you. What's more,' he said, 'that artist was murdered and I can prove it. I have insights that your local village idiot of a copper doesn't have.' "

"Did you tell anyone what he had said?"

"I was that furious, I told a lot of people. Bessie came in for a coffee, and I told her."

"Bessie! Man, you might as well have put up a neon sign in the village."

"How was I to know he'd go and get himself kilt? I mean, everyone was saying thon artist committed suicide."

"Weren't the police up here during the night asking everyone about Hal?"

"Aye, but I was off duty, so they didn't ask me. I suppose they only interviewed the staff who live in."

Hamish went out into the main area of the hotel and into the manager's office.

"This is a bad business," said Mr. Johnson.

"Have the guests been checking out?"

"Not yet. But most of them won't have heard anything. It's too early."

"Clarry said Mr. Addenfest was in the kitchen in the early evening complaining about his packed lunch. Did he come to see you?"

"I didn't know he had even returned to the hotel. He may have left by the kitchen door."

Hamish went back to Clarry. "Did Addenfest leave by the kitchen door?"

"Aye, he slammed out. Nearly took the door off its hinges."

Hamish thanked him and then went back and asked Mr. Johnson which room Jock was in.

"He's not paying, so we put him up in one of the attic rooms. It's number sixty-two. We only put guests in there if we're fully booked and they insist on staying.

141

Hardly room to swing a cat."

Hamish went up to the top of the castle, located Jock's attic room, and knocked on the door. He waited. There was no reply. Suddenly anxious, he tried the handle. The door was unlocked. He opened it and went in.

There were two figures wrapped around each other on a single bed. One was Jock, and the other was the maid, Bessie.

Chapter Seven

To see her is to love her,
And love but her forever,
For Nature made her what she is,
And ne'er made anither!
— Robert Burns

Hamish was about to retreat when Bessie woke up suddenly, saw him, and let out a scream. Jock awoke at the sound and struggled up against the pillows.

"I'll see you downstairs in the lounge, Jock," said Hamish.

Hamish sat in the lounge and began to wonder if he had been gravely wrong in his assessment of Jock's character. Jock had seemed to him like an easy-going man, only interested in his work.

Betty Barnard entered the lounge. "Hamish! What brings you here?"

"I want a word with Jock. He'll be down any minute."

"Mind if I stay?"

"I would like a word with him in private."

"I *am* his agent."

"But not his lawyer," said Hamish. "Please, Betty."

"I heard that American had been found dead."

"Yes."

"So what's that got to do with Jock?"

"I've got to check where anyone connected with Effie was last night."

"What's the death of this American got to do with Effie?"

"Here's Jock," said Hamish. "I'll talk to you later."

Betty went off, and Jock sat down opposite Hamish. "I know it looks bad," he said. "But it gets a bit lonely up here."

Hamish raised his eyebrows. "I would have thought with your agent being here and your ex-wife in Lochdubh, not to mention painting Priscilla, that you'd have enough company."

"Come on, Hamish. I felt like a wee bit of sex, and the lassie was willing."

"Where were you the night before last?"

"Let me see. I had dinner in the hotel with Betty. We stayed up late, and then we went to our rooms. She'll confirm it."

"I'm surprised Effie knew where

Geordie's Cleft was."

"She probably asked someone."

Her mobile phone, thought Hamish suddenly. I can't remember anyone ever finding her phone. He stood up. "That'll be all for now, Jock, but don't leave Lochdubh."

"It was a suicide. Can't you leave it alone?"

"Hal Addenfest, the American who was staying here, was murdered. I think the two deaths are connected."

Hamish left the lounge, leaving Jock staring after him.

To Hamish's dismay, Jimmy Anderson, followed by police and detectives, entered the hotel. Jimmy was brandishing a search warrant.

"Do you have to do this?" asked Hamish, thinking uneasily of the effect on the hotel guests and subsequently on Priscilla. The guests may not have bothered to check out when they heard the news of the murder, but he was afraid a lot of them would do so after getting their rooms searched.

" 'Fraid so," said Jimmy, knocking at the manager's door. "He was hit with some sort of blunt weapon. He stayed here. We've got to look."

"There was no blood around his head,"

said Hamish. "Was he killed elsewhere? Did forensic find anything?"

"Yes, their little bloodshot eyes found a patch of blood further up the beach. Nothing else. That shingle won't hold footprints. They had to work fast before the tide covered everything up as far as the seawall. Want to join in the search?"

"I think I'll go back down to the village. The locals might tell me things they wouldnae tell you."

Elspeth Grant, who worked for the *Bugle* in Glasgow, was summoned by her news editor as soon as she got into the office.

"There's a murder in Lochdubh," he said. "Some American tourist. I want you to get up there right away."

"But Matthew Campbell, who's now the local reporter, covers that area. You know he's good. He used to work for you."

"He's been getting sloppy since he was married. You know the area, you know the local copper, get home and pack a bag and get off as fast as possible."

"I'll take a plane to Inverness and hire a car once I get there." Elspeth hoped the news editor would argue about the expense and maybe decide that, after all, the coverage should be left to Matthew. But he said, "Well, what are you waiting for?"

Elspeth did not want to see Hamish Macbeth again. She had been in love with him, and he had rejected her. The hurt had been deep, and so she had refused to accept any phone calls from him.

She was able to pack a bag, drive to the airport, and book herself on the eleven o'clock plane to Inverness. At the airport, having left her own car at Glasgow airport, she hired a car and set out for Sutherland.

She drove steadily up towards Lochdubh, her anger at the job dissipating as she found herself once more back over the highland line.

Elspeth decided to book in at the Tommel Castle Hotel. She hoped any story she might get would be worth all this expense.

Hamish started off by going again to see the two boys who had found the body. He guessed, rightly as it turned out, that they would be kept out of school to recover from their shock.

They were evidently beginning to feel excited and important, but they had nothing further to add. Sean said he thought he had heard the plop of a seal diving out on the lake, but that was all either of them had to add.

Hamish then went from house to house, questioning one after the other, only breaking off to go back to the police station to feed the dog and cat and take them for a walk. No one had seen anything, and most were cross at being questioned by Hamish when they had already been questioned by police.

Jimmy called in at the police station in the early evening. "I'm knackered — and that police cell bed last night was as hard as hell," he said. "I'm off home. We'll all start first thing tomorrow and go over everything again. There was nothing sinister in any of the rooms. We've got the police in Glasgow checking up on those three — Jock, his ex-wife, and his agent. Brighton police are looking into the sister's background. I may have some results tomorrow. From what I gather from the guests, this Hal Addenfest was a right pill. Maybe someone ran into him by moonlight on the beach and picked up a rock and hit him with it."

"He must have walked down there to meet someone," said Hamish. "His car's still at the hotel. He wouldnae go down there in the middle o' the night for no reason at all."

"Well, we'll see. I'm off."

Hamish changed out of his police uniform and showered, then dressed in a pair of old corduroy trousers and faded tartan shirt.

He went out to the deep freeze in the shed and was rooting around to see if there was something for his dinner when he heard a car arriving. He walked out of the shed and found to his delight that it was Betty.

The last rays of sun were glinting on the blonde streaks in her hair. She was wearing a dark blue silk trouser suit and high heels.

"Hullo, copper," she said. "I thought you might like a meal out, so I'll take you to the Italian's if you're free."

"That would be grand," said Hamish. "Come in, and I'll dress in something better. I've still got a report to send over, but I can do it later."

He was in the bedroom changing into his one good suit when he heard someone else arrive. He finished dressing quickly and went into the kitchen. Priscilla was sitting at the table with Betty.

"I thought you might like some dinner, Hamish," said Priscilla, indicating a casserole on the table. "But Betty tells me you are going out for dinner, so you can put it in the fridge and have it tomorrow."

Because of the warm evening, the kitchen door was open. Elspeth Grant walked in.

Hamish stared at her. Her hair, which had been straightened the last time he had seen her, was now back to its usual frizzy style. Her silver eyes — Gypsy eyes — surveyed him and then the two women at the table.

"I'm up covering the murder," said Elspeth. "I was going to take you for a meal, but I see you have company."

"This is Betty Barnard," said Priscilla in a cool voice. "Betty is a guest at the hotel. We are both too late. Betty is taking Hamish for dinner. Go ahead, Hamish. We'll let ourselves out."

"See you," said Betty cheerfully. "Come along, Hamish."

There was a long silence after Hamish had left. Then Priscilla said, "I brought him this casserole. Shame if it goes to waste. Why don't we both have dinner?"

"All right," said Elspeth. "Is that woman going to be Mrs. Macbeth?"

"Betty? No, I shouldn't think so. She's an artists' agent. Her client is Jock Fleming."

"Who is Jock Fleming?"

"I'll pop this in the oven, and I've got a bottle of wine here," said Priscilla. "We'll have a drink, and I'll tell you all about it."

Elspeth felt intimidated by Priscilla, watching her as she moved about the kitchen with quiet efficiency. Priscilla was wearing tailored white linen trousers with a white linen blouse. Elspeth reflected that when she wore anything made of linen, it seemed to crease as soon as she got it on, but Priscilla's ensemble showed not a wrinkle, and her hair was smooth and golden. Elspeth nervously dragged her fingers through her own hair trying to flatten it and only succeeded in making it look messier than ever.

Priscilla opened the wine and poured two glasses. "The casserole will only take a few minutes. Right, I'll begin at the beginning . . ."

Hamish did not enjoy his dinner. He kept wondering what Priscilla and Elspeth were talking about. Seeing Elspeth again had been a shock.

"I keep asking you how the investigation is going on," said Betty, "and you mumble something but don't seem to be listening. I know about Priscilla. The whole of Lochdubh knows about Priscilla, but

151

who's the other one?"

"A reporter, Elspeth Grant. She used to work on the paper here."

"And?"

"And what?"

"Were you romantically involved with her?"

Hamish stiffened. Betty, amused, thought if Hamish were a cat, his fur would stand on end. "I haff neffer asked you about your private life, Betty," he said, "and I don't wish to discuss mine."

"Okay, Sherlock. Now we've got that out of the way, have you any suspects?"

"I'm waiting until all the background on everyone comes in," said Hamish.

"Me included?"

"I should think so. You and everyone else staying at the hotel."

"I'm a clean-living girl. They can dig away. I'm surprised you're free for dinner. I thought your bosses would be hounding you."

"No. That scunner, Detective Chief Inspector Blair, is laid up in hospital with a broken leg and a broken collarbone, and Detective Jimmy Anderson is in charge of the case. He knows it's pointless now to go over old ground until we know more about the people involved. Nice not to be harassed."

152

"Macbeth," said a voice behind him.

Hamish swung round and looked up at the figure of Superintendent Peter Daviot looming over him. Hamish got to his feet.

"Why aren't you out on the case?" asked Daviot.

"Because, sir, everyone's been pretty much interviewed and Anderson is waiting for the background checks."

"I'm sorry to spoil your dinner, but I want you to walk along to the police station with me. There is a lot to discuss." He smiled at Betty. "I am sorry, miss, but this is serious stuff."

Betty gave a little shrug. "Don't mind me."

At least Priscilla and Elspeth will have left, thought Hamish. But when he opened the kitchen door, it was to find the pair finishing their meal.

Daviot knew them both and murmured a greeting while a flustered Hamish explained he would have to ask them to leave.

Priscilla asked after Mrs. Daviot as she efficiently cleared the table and put the dirty dishes and glasses in the sink. Then she and Elspeth left.

Daviot sat down at the table. Sonsie

jumped onto the chair opposite and fixed the superintendent with unblinking eyes.

"Good heavens, Macbeth. That's a wild cat. You shouldn't be keeping an animal like that!"

"She's domesticated." Hamish lifted his cat down onto the floor and sat down opposite Daviot.

"Now, this business of a murdered American tourist is serious," said Daviot. "This sort of thing can damage tourism. We have contacted his ex-wife, who is flying over to make funeral arrangements. He had a card in his wallet with her mobile phone number. We could not find any close family. Have you any idea why he was murdered?"

"Yes," said Hamish. "It all ties in with the murder of Effie Garrard."

"The artist? But that was suicide."

"I think not, sir." Hamish explained about the visitors to Effie's cottage and about the bottle of wine and the note.

"I never saw any report about that note or bottle of wine."

"Her sister, Caro, who is up here, told the police in Strathbane, but they said Effie was mad and had probably made the whole thing up."

Daviot scowled. "I'll see about this when

I get back to headquarters. So what ties Effie to this American?"

"He took her out a couple of times. He had ambitions to be a writer, and he noted down everything everyone had said in a notebook. I asked to see what she had said, and Mr. Addenfest replied that he knew the police thought it was suicide but he had proof that it was murder and would only show the contents to my superiors."

"And why didn't you report this?"

"Because I was told the case was closed and to leave it alone."

"And there's no sign of the notebook?"

"No, not on the body or in his room."

Daviot rapped his fingers on the table, an irritating sound. Then he said, "We have a new detective constable, Robin Mackenzie."

"What's he like?"

"*She*. Keen as mustard. I want her to work closely on this case with you, and I want you to give her the benefit of all your local knowledge. Anderson will handle the broad picture, and I will be in charge."

"When does this detective arrive?"

"I asked her to report to you first thing tomorrow morning. We must all work night and day on this. No time off for anyone." He glanced at his watch. "I'd better go. I have a late-night party to attend at the Freemasons. Then tomorrow morning, I have to get my new suit from the tailor. I'll be over in the afternoon to see how you're getting on."

"I do not want to be obstructive, sir, but would not this Detective Mackenzie be better working with Anderson? I work better alone."

"You what? This isn't the Wild West with a lone sheriff. Do as you're told and give Mackenzie all the help she needs."

After Daviot left, Hamish felt quite low. The case was difficult enough without being saddled with some pushy woman detective. He assumed first thing in the morning meant around nine o'clock. He set the alarm for eight and went to bed, feeling mildly hungry because he'd only eaten the first course before Daviot had taken him away, but felt too tired to cook anything.

Hamish was awakened at six in the morning by a banging on the front door. He struggled out of bed, went to the door, and shouted, "Come round to the kitchen."

He put on a dressing gown and went and opened the kitchen door.

"I'm Robin Mackenzie," said his visitor.

"Come ben. What time d'ye call this?"

"I was instructed to report early."

Robin Mackenzie was a fairly small woman with dark brown hair worn in a French pleat. She had small dark brown eyes, a long straight nose, and a wide mouth. She was wearing a white blouse, suede jacket, and tweed skirt. Her black patent leather shoes had low heels.

"You are not what I expected," she said, looking up at the tall, unshaven figure of Hamish with his flaming red hair tousled from sleep.

"What did you expect?" asked Hamish.

"Someone fully dressed and in uniform, for a start."

"I'll make you some coffee and get dressed."

The dog and the cat wandered in. She looked at them but made no comment, and thank goodness for that, thought Hamish.

When the coffee was ready, he served her a mug of it and took himself off to the bathroom to shower and shave.

Robin looked around the kitchen. She had grown up in South Uist in the Outer Hebrides and had left as soon as she could to fulfil her ambition of becoming a detective. She had heard reports of Hamish's brilliance and how he always managed to avoid promotion, and she had wondered why. Being stuck in a highland police station out in the wilds, she thought, would be as bad as being back in South Uist.

She thought Hamish was probably some eccentric and the stories about him had been wild exaggerations. Hadn't Blair often told her that Macbeth was some highland idiot who just occasionally got lucky?

Hamish came back, dressed in his uniform, and said, "Just a minute. I've got to let my hens out."

Robin suppressed an exclamation of irritation.

When he returned, Hamish then fussed about filling up the animals' water bowls. When he finished, Robin said impatiently, "Can we get started?"

"I've got to walk my beasts. Come with me, and we can talk as we go along."

I should have brought a camera, thought Robin. No one would ever believe this.

As they strolled along the waterfront, Hamish told her everything he had found out.

After he had finished, he said, "I thought we might go up and see the sister, Caro Garrard. You question her, and I'll see if there is any variation in her statement. Then we'll try some of the others. It's ower early. We'll need to wait a bit until folks wake up."

Nessie and Jessie Currie peered through their net curtains. "He's got a lassie with him," said Nessie. "Oh, my, she must have spent the night. She should be warned."

"Warned," echoed Jessie.

Robin noticed that two small women were approaching them. Hairnets covered their tightly permed hair, and they were wearing identical dressing gowns over flannel men's pyjamas. On their feet, each wore a pair of Snoopy slippers. The morning sun glinted off their glasses.

Hamish saw them and said hurriedly, "Let's get back to the police station."

"Not so fast!" shouted Nessie.

"So fast," echoed her sister.

Hamish groaned and stopped. "Young woman," said Nessie, "they may have loose morals in the cities, but in Lochdubh, we are decent, God-fearing people."

"I am Detective Robin Mackenzie," said Robin, her fluting South Uist accent cutting through Jessie's usual echo. "I arrived at the police station at six o'clock this morning to begin work. Now, what can I do for you?"

"Just came out to say welcome," mumbled Nessie, and the twins bolted back towards their cottage.

"If the rest of the inhabitants are as deranged as that pair, I'm not surprised there have been two murders up here," said Robin.

"They're very nice women," said Hamish defensively. He hated any of the inhabitants being criticised by outsiders.

They walked back to the police station. "I'll fix us an omelette for breakfast," said Hamish.

In the kitchen, Robin noticed that the cat and dog stared at each other for a long moment and then slouched out. "Where are they going?" she asked.

"Who?"

"Your cat and dog."

"I don't know," said Hamish crossly, lifting the lid of the stove and dropping in slices of brown peat. He knew exactly where they had gone. They had gone back to his bed to continue sleeping, but he did not want to tell her that.

"I'm chust going out to get some eggs," he said.

Bloody women, thought Hamish as he collected fresh eggs from the hen house. I'm surrounded by them.

He returned to the kitchen and began to beat up the eggs for an omelette.

Robin watched him. Her heart was sinking rapidly. She should be out there with the experts, not stuck in this kitchen with this lanky policeman and his weird cat and weirder dog.

The omelette was excellent but the coffee dreadful. She edged her cup aside.

"I'll make us some tea," said Hamish. "That coffee's a disgrace, and so I shall tell Patel."

"Is it instant?"

"Yes, it's called High Mountain Blue. It was on special offer. I think it's made from the sweepings on the floor after they've processed the real stuff. After we see Caro, the sister, I think we should pay a visit to the seer, Angus Macdonald."

This is truly awful, thought Robin. I'm stuck with a copper who believes in clairvoyants.

Hamish saw the expression on her face and grinned. "Angus is an old fraud, but he bases his so-called predictions and insights on listening closely to gossip."

Caro Garrard looked at them wearily when they arrived on her doorstep. "More questions?"

"Just a few," said Hamish amiably. "May we come in? This is Detective Mackenzie."

"Don't be long," Caro said. "I slept badly last night, and I was planning to go back to bed."

They sat down round the work table. Hamish removed his cap. A sunbeam shone on the rich red of his hair. I wonder if he dyes it, thought Robin. She cleared her throat and took out her notebook.

She took Caro over everything she had told Hamish. Caro wearily replied to her questions. Then Robin asked, "Just how furious were you when you discovered she had been passing your art off as her own?"

"I was very angry," said Caro. "Oh, it wasn't just that. It was an accumulation of all her other troubles I'd had to put up with. I sometimes think I would be married now if she hadn't messed things up for me. No, I didn't kill her. That murder wasn't done by someone in a hot rage. It was cold and calculating."

"I think she did it," said Robin as they got back into the Land Rover.

"Why?" asked Hamish.

"She was calculating enough to initially hide the fact that she was not in Brighton but up here, having it out with Effie."

162

"We'll see." Hamish drove in the direction of the seer's cottage. He stopped the car at the foot of a hill and said, "We'll need to get out and walk. His cottage is up there." Angus's cottage was perched on the top of a hill with a winding path leading up to it.

The seer opened the door to them just as they arrived on his doorstep. "Come ben," he said. "What have you brought me?"

Hamish had forgotten that Angus always expected a present. "I haven't had time," he said. "We're in the middle of an investigation. Look, I'll get you a salmon later."

"A real one out o' the river," ordered Angus, "and not one o' thae ones out o' the fish farm."

Robin looked around the living room curiously. It was a low-ceiling room with an armchair on one side of the fire and two ladder-back Orkney chairs on the other. There was a table covered with the remains of breakfast by the small window set deep into the thick stone wall. The air was scented with peat smoke from the smouldering fire. Angus put an old blackened kettle on a hook over the fire. Hamish knew the seer had a perfectly good electric kettle in the kitchen but used the old-fashioned way of boiling water to impress visitors.

Angus sat down in the armchair, and Robin and Hamish took the chairs on the other side of the fire. "And who is this young lady?" asked Angus, stroking his long grey beard.

"I am Robin Mackenzie," she said. "I am a detective who has been sent up here to work closely with Constable Macbeth."

"And hating every minute of it," said Angus. "Poor wee lassie sitting there thinking, what am I doing stuck here with this loon?"

Robin's face flamed. "Nothing of the kind."

Angus heaved himself to his feet. "Kettle's boiled. I'll just get the cups and an ashtray for you, Miss Mackenzie."

"I don't smoke!"

"Yes, you do," said Angus, disappearing into the kitchen.

Hamish looked amused. "Is he right?"

"I'm trying to give up," said Robin. "Oh, what the hell." She took off her jacket and, rolling up the sleeve of her blouse, ripped off a nicotine patch and threw it on the fire. She replaced her jacket, opened her handbag, and took out a packet of Bensons. Hamish watched hungrily as she lit one up. He had given up smoking a long time ago, but the craving for a cigarette had never quite left him.

Angus made tea and poured cups and then, when they were served, sat down again. "You've come about the murder of that artist," he said.

Robin started. "So you think that was murder?"

"Oh, aye."

"So who did it?"

Angus closed his eyes. "I see four people circling around her like the buzzards. I see . . ."

Robin leaned forward expectantly but the seer only emitted a gentle snore.

"Come on," said Hamish. "We won't be getting any more out of him today."

"Where now?" asked Robin.

Hamish stared down the hill to the village. "I see a mobile police unit has been set up. Time to visit Jimmy and see what he's found out."

As the Land Rover bumped over the heathery hill tracks towards the village, Robin wondered uneasily what Hamish had thought of the seer's accurate reading of her thoughts. She was beginning to sense a sharp intelligence behind Hamish's laconic manner and feared she had misjudged him.

"That remark of Angus's about me thinking you stupid was not correct," she said.

"Oh, it probably was," said Hamish. "Don't worry about it."

He drove along the waterfront and parked in front of the mobile unit.

He and Robin mounted the shallow steps and went in. Jimmy Anderson was sitting behind a desk studying a computer. "You're just in time, Hamish. What are you doing here, Robin?"

"Superintendent Daviot has asked me to work with Hamish."

"He has, has he? Both of you come and look at this." He handed them a computer printout.

It was a statement about Jock Fleming. On two occasions, he had been charged with assault and drunk and disorderly. One of the charges concerned his wife. She had used as grounds for divorce his attack on her where he has broken two of her ribs.

"I'm slipping," mourned Hamish. "I thought that man was just an ordinary cheerful chap. Will we go and see him?"

"No, I'll do that," Jimmy said.

"Any other horrible news?"

"The ex-wife used to be a hooker and a drug addict."

"Michty me! Anything else?"

"Caro Garrard had a nervous breakdown, but it was a long time ago, just after she left art school. I'd like you both to go and see Dora Fleming. Find out why she was lying. Find out why she is pursuing a violent ex-husband."

"Where does this woman live?" asked Robin as they left the mobile unit.

"A boarding house, just along the waterfront here."

"What's she like?"

"Defiant, coarse, sometimes a really broad Glasgow accent and sometimes it's modified."

"Who's this bulldog in tweed bearing down on us?" asked Robin.

"Mrs. Wellington, the minister's wife."

"Hamish Macbeth," boomed Mrs. Wellington, "just who is this female?"

"Manners," chided Hamish. "Robin, may I present Mrs. Wellington. Mrs. Wellington, Detective Constable Mackenzie."

"That's all right, then," said Mrs. Wellington. "I thought for a moment you were playing fast and loose with another female."

"Are they all like that in this village?" asked Robin. "I mean, is it inbreeding or something?"

"Chust bloody-minded nosiness, that's all."

"Hamish!" called a voice.

Hamish swung round. Elspeth came hurrying along the waterfront. She was wearing jeans and a faded T-shirt. "We should get together soon," said Elspeth.

Hamish introduced Robin and then said, "I honestly don't know when I'll be free."

"You owe me some of your time," said Elspeth.

"Call round at the police station at nine this evening," said Hamish. "I should be through by then."

Elspeth's odd silver eyes surveyed him. "Enjoy your dinner?"

"Yes, thank you. Now, if you don't mind . . ."

"Enjoy it while supplies last," said Elspeth. "There's misery coming from that quarter."

Hamish made a sound of disgust and walked on rapidly. Robin hurried to keep up with him.

"What on earth was she talking about?"

"Oh, she thinks she's psychic."

"Really? I hope we're nearly at this boarding house. I've had enough of nutters for one day."

But at the boarding house, Mrs. Dunne

168

said Mrs. Fleming had decided to walk up to the Tommel Castle Hotel to see her ex-husband.

"Why, I wonder?" said Hamish. "We'd better drive up there, Robin."

When they reached the hotel, Hamish said, "I'll get Mr. Johnson to send someone up to fetch her down here. I don't want to end up stepping on Jimmy's toes."

Mr. Johnson told them to wait in the lounge. There was no sign of Bessie, the maid. Hamish decided to interview her later.

Dora Fleming came in and slumped down in an armchair opposite them.

"You lied to me," said Hamish.

"Whit?"

"You got a divorce from Jock because he had been beating you."

"So I didnae like to tell folks that while he's paying alimony."

"And why did you really come up here?"

"He was behind a bit wi' the payments. It's all right now."

"Why are you still here and visiting him, too?" asked Robin.

"He's the faither o' ma weans."

"How did you meet him?" asked Hamish.

The heavy accent dropped from her voice as she said, with a toss of her head, "It was at a gallery opening in Glasgow."

"So it was not while you were working as a prostitute?" asked Robin.

Hamish had heard of people's eyes turning red with rage and had put that description down to poetic license, but now he could swear he saw red glints of fury in Dora's eyes.

"You bastards!" she howled. "You never let a body alone to lead a decent life."

"How did you meet Jock?" asked Hamish patiently.

"It *was* at a gallery opening," she said sulkily. "A man friend — okay, a client — was a bit drunk, and when we was finished, he said he'd take me to a party. That's where I met Jock at the gallery. He said he'd like to do a portrait of me."

Hamish surveyed her. "I thought Jock only painted landscapes and that this portrait of Miss Halburton-Smythe was a one-off."

Dora gave a contemptuous sniff. "That agent o' his told him to stick to landscapes because portraits werenae his thing, but Jock said it was a good chat-up line."

I must see Priscilla, thought Hamish anxiously. If Angela is right and jealousy

170

was behind the murder of Effie, then she could be at risk. Or if Jock did it, she'll still be at risk.

He got to his feet. "Could you carry on with the questioning, Robin?"

Robin looked at him severely. "And just where do you think you are going?"

"I've got to pee," said Hamish.

He headed toward the door. Now for Priscilla.

CHAPTER EIGHT

*She may very well pass for forty-three
In the dusk with a light behind her!*
— W. S. Gilbert

Priscilla was crossing the reception area when Hamish stopped her. "It's urgent," he said.

"All right. Let's go into the lounge."

"No, not there. Robin's interviewing Jock's wife."

"Who's he?"

"*She*. A detective."

"Let's use the office, then. Mr. Johnson's gone out shopping." Priscilla selected a key from a whole bunch of them on a chain fastened around her slim waist.

"You look like the chatelaine of the castle. Do you have to work? Where are your parents?"

"They've gone to visit the Derwents over in Caithness. I don't mind."

She unlocked the door. "Help yourself to

coffee and tell me what it's all about."

Hamish poured himself a mug from the coffee machine in the corner and turned and raised an eyebrow. "Not for me," said Priscilla.

"It's like this," said Hamish. "We were interviewing Jock's ex-wife. She says Jock only offers to paint a woman's portrait as a way of chatting her up."

"He seems harmless enough, Hamish. I'm vain enough to want this portrait."

"Priscilla, he's got a record of assault. Angela Brodie had an idea that maybe jealousy was behind these murders. If that is the reason Effie was killed, then you could be next."

"I don't think so," said Priscilla with maddening calm. "The portrait seems to be coming along all right. He's just a large, friendly man. His only interest in me is as a subject."

"I neffer thought of you as being naïve," said Hamish.

The door of the office opened, and Robin's voice said sharply, "What are you doing, Hamish? Jimmy has taken Jock off to the police unit for further questioning, and he wants us there."

Hamish turned in the doorway. "Remember what I said, Priscilla."

"Remember what?" asked Robin as they got into the Land Rover.

Hamish told her about his fears.

When he finished, Robin said, "So you think the murderer might have been a woman?"

"It's possible. I think that ex-wife of his could be capable of murder."

At the mobile police unit, they found Jimmy questioning Jock. "You see why we are so suspicious," said Jimmy. "You lied first time round. What's to say you aren't lying again?"

"I've told you and told you," said Jock. "I had a late dinner with Betty, and then we both went to our respective rooms. That would be around eleven o'clock in the evening."

Robin studied Jock while the questioning went on. She could see what attracted women to this apparently friendly bear of a man. At one point in the questioning, he looked across at her and made a funny face, and she had to bite her lip to stop herself from bursting out laughing.

"You seem friendly enough with your ex-wife," Hamish said.

"Och, I never was one to keep resentments. She's the mother of my children.

She's a good mother."

"So why isn't she back in Glasgow with them?"

"She needs a holiday, and the children are being well looked after by her mother."

"How did you first meet Dora?" asked Robin.

"Some party in a gallery. We hit it off right away."

"Did you know right away she was a prostitute?"

"She told me. It didn't matter. I was keen on her."

Hamish studied Jock. His eyes seemed clear and honest as he turned to look at each one of them in turn.

"You didn't know," said Hamish flatly. He had never trusted anyone who looked at him with that straight, unblinking gaze. "She moved in with you right away. You didn't know until after she got you to marry her. The first assault on her was when you found out."

Jock suddenly lost his temper. "Dora promised not to say a word!"

"The truth, please," said Jimmy.

"I don't see what this has to do with anything. Oh, all right. We'd been to the theatre and went for a late-night meal. We were walking along Bath Street when this

175

hoor steps out of a doorway and cries, 'Why, Dora! Haven't seen you in ages. You got a different beat?'

"Dora hurried me past the woman. I waited until we got home and demanded an answer. She only came out with the truth after I hit her. She said she was tired of the streets and had seen me as an easy mark. She had deliberately got pregnant so that I would marry her. Then the bitch got to the phone and called the police and reported me for assault."

"So why didn't you divorce her then?"

"I was too busy to be bothered."

"And you went ahead and had another child," said Hamish. "You must ha' cared for her enough."

"Well, I was right sorry I had hit her. Things seemed to settle down to normal. Then she said there was another woman. I told her that was rubbish. She began turning up at parties and galleries and accusing me of adultery."

"And that's when you assaulted her again?"

"Yes. She was making a fool of me."

"Was there another woman?"

"No. It was all in her stupid head. I told her I wanted a divorce and if she didn't give me one, I'd tell everyone about her having been a prostitute. So she agreed.

What the hell she was doing telling you about her background is beyond me."

"Don't go beating her up again," said Hamish. "She didn't tell us much. We knew from police reports that she'd been a prostitute. I guessed the rest."

Jimmy resumed the questioning. Jock stuck to his story about calling on Effie the evening she disappeared. He said he had then gone back to the hotel and had a late dinner with Betty. He said he had seen the American around the hotel but hadn't talked to him.

Hamish thought that strange. He had been under the impression that Hal had buttonholed everyone.

After the questioning was over, Jock was dismissed but told not to leave Lochdubh.

"You two had better go and check his alibi with his agent," said Jimmy.

Robin and Hamish got back into the Land Rover.

"How on earth did you guess that Jock had not known Dora was a prostitute when he married her?" asked Robin.

"People from Glasgow can never lie like a highlander," said Hamish. "His shoulders were stiff. And when anyone turns a clear, unblinking, honest gaze on me, I know they're lying."

"What's this agent, Betty Barnard, like? Oh, look! A heron." She pointed.

They had almost reached the end of the waterfront. Hamish slowed the vehicle. A heron was standing over a rocky pool on its long thin legs, gazing down into the water. Its beak suddenly flashed down into the water and came up with a fish. It rose majestically into the air, lazily flapping its huge wings, and soared up over the loch.

"Fish sometimes get trapped in the pools at low tide," said Hamish, speeding up again.

"I was asking you what Betty Barnard was like."

"Very nice. She's by way of being a friend of mine."

"Don't let that stop you suspecting her," Robin warned.

Mr. Johnson, the manager, back from his shopping, told them that Betty was out somewhere. Hamish and Robin took seats in the bar where they could sit and watch through the open door into the reception area.

"Would you like a drink?" asked Hamish.

"I'll have an orange juice." Hamish ordered orange juice for her and coffee for himself.

Half an hour passed. They were just about to give up when Betty walked into reception. Hamish hailed her.

Betty was wearing another trouser suit, a silky thing the same green as her eyes. "I was down at the police station looking for you, Hamish," she said. "I called in at that police unit, and they told me I'd find you up here because you wanted to question me."

"Can I get you anything to drink?" asked Hamish.

"A gin and tonic with a lot of ice would be lovely. I took your beasts out for a walk and fed them. They're all right."

Hamish looked at her in genuine gratitude. "Thanks a lot, Betty. They're worse than children."

He called to the barman, "A gin and tonic over here. Lots of ice. Now, Betty . . ."

"I'll do the questioning," said Robin firmly. "Miss Barnard . . ."

"Betty, please."

"Betty. Let's go over again the evening Effie disappeared. You said you met Mr. Fleming for a late dinner. What were you doing earlier in the evening?"

"Let me see. I have other artists, you know. I was up in my room making phone calls. You can check my hotel phone bill."

"We'll need to check your mobile as well."

"You'll need to go to Glasgow to do that. I left it behind."

"Give me your mobile phone number."

Betty did and raised her eyebrows at Hamish as if wondering why he was letting Robin ask all the questions.

"So you were in your room for the early part of the evening. Any witnesses?"

"Yes, that maid, Bessie something or other. I ordered a drink from room service, and she brought it up."

"What time was that?"

"Not sure. About eight o'clock."

The bar had begun to fill up. "Press," explained Hamish. "They're all over the place. Let's move to the lounge." He saw Matthew Campbell among the reporters and photographers and made a mental note to call on him later and see if he had found out anything.

Once seated in a corner of the lounge, Robin started the questioning again.

"So did you meet Jock for dinner by previous arrangement?"

"No, he called on me in my room and said he'd been up to see Effie. He told me he had straightened her out and said he was famished."

"What time was this?"

"It was about nine o'clock. I said we'd better hurry down to the dining room because they stopped cooking at nine-thirty."

"And when did you finish eating?"

"Around eleven. Then we went to our respective rooms."

"Did you know Jock Fleming before he was married?"

"Yes. A friend introduced us and begged me to look at his work. I did. I saw it was marketable. People are turning away from abstracts. I arranged an exhibition for him, and he did very well indeed. He's not top of the market yet, but if you want a Jock Fleming landscape, it'll set you back ten thousand pounds. He's a coming lad."

"What did you think about his marriage?"

"I was a bit surprised. I thought her a coarse little thing. But he was so happy about the baby coming, and he was working harder than ever. Besides, it's not my job to interfere in the personal life of my artists."

"And yet you came all the way up here to be with him?"

"I needed a holiday, and I wanted to protect my investment. Jock was my first big success."

The interview went on. Betty answered all Robin's questions simply and directly.

After Robin had finished, Hamish said, "I'd like a word with Betty alone, if you don't mind."

"I'll wait for you outside," said Robin.

"It's like this, Betty," said Hamish awkwardly. "Now that this is an official murder case, I can't afford to socialise with you until the murderer is found. I'm right grateful to you for looking after the animals, but you see how it is."

She gave him a warm smile. "Don't worry, Hamish. Catch your murderer, and we'll have a party to celebrate."

Hamish joined Robin outside. "Before we leave here, we should have a word with the maid, Bessie Jamieson."

"Why?"

"I caught her in bed with Jock. Maybe he said something useful to her."

Back in the hotel, Mr. Johnson summoned Bessie. "You can use my office," he said. "Don't be too long about it. Bessie's got work to do. A lot of the guests have left, but they've been replaced by the gentlemen of the press."

"Sit down, Bessie," said Hamish. She was a plump girl with shiny brown hair and rosy cheeks. "Now, you went to bed with Jock Fleming."

182

"It was just a wee bit o' fun, Hamish."

"I'm sure it was. Did he say anything to you that might have a bearing on the death of Effie Garrard?"

"Let me see. He'd ordered a bottle of whisky, and I took it up to him. He asked me to join him. We got drinking and talking. He said he'd like to paint me. He said Effie had been chasing him and she'd been a pain in the neck, but that was all. We got a wee bit drunk and he started kissing me and afore I knew it, we were in bed."

"And has he spoken to you since?"

"He said it wouldn't be a good idea, what with his wife being up here. I said okay, cos I've got a boyfriend down in Inverness. Och, it didnae mean anything."

"And he didn't say anything else about that American or Effie?"

"Not that I can bring to mind."

"If you think of anything, Bessie, phone me right away."

"Are there really women like that?" asked Robin after Bessie had left.

"Like what?"

"I mean, just hop into bed with a man and forget it next day?"

"Don't ask me," said Hamish. "They havenae exactly come my way. Who do you want to interview next?"

"I'd like something to eat first."

"Let's go to the police station," said Hamish. "I've got a couple of trout in the freezer."

"Okay. Then I'd like to interview the biggest gossip in the village."

"Hard to tell. When it comes to gossip, they're all on an equal footing. Maybe, though, the Currie sisters have the edge."

After lunch, Hamish led Robin to the Currie sisters' cottage. He was not looking forward to the interview, knowing that both sisters regarded him as a sort of Lothario.

Strangely enough, Nessie was alone. Hamish could hardly remember a time when he had found the twin sisters separated from each other.

"Jessie's gone up to the church to do the flowers," said Nessie, her already wrinkled face creasing in disapproval. "I don't hold with flowers in church. It smacks of popery. What do you want?"

"Detective Mackenzie here would like to ask you a few questions."

"Don't be long. I'm right tired of answering questions. I suppose you'll be wanting tea, Macbeth."

"No, thank you. We've just eaten."

184

"He's just saying that because you're here," said Nessie to Robin. "Hamish Macbeth is the biggest moocher for miles around. Sit down. I won't be long."

They both sat down in the neat little living room. The windows were open, allowing a gentle breeze scented with pine into the room. The only good thing about taking tea with the Curries, thought Hamish, was that it was served on the round table by the window and not on a coffee table. He was very tall and disliked bending double over low coffee tables to take tea.

Nessie came back with a tray laden with tea and scones. "Help yourself," she said. They gathered around the table.

"Eat something first," Nessie ordered Robin. "You've got to keep your strength up. A young lassie like you should be getting married and having bairns."

The scones were feather light and generously filled with butter and strawberry jam.

Robin dutifully ate one, took a sip of tea, and said, "I know you've been asked this question before, but I thought that perhaps you might have remembered something new. Did you see anyone on the waterfront the night Mr. Addenfest was killed?"

"We mind our own business, me and Jessie."

"I am sure you do. But you are such a sharp-eyed and intelligent woman that I was sure you might have noticed something that nobody else would think important."

Hamish was amused to notice the struggle between vanity and ignorance on Nessie's face. Nessie was obviously delighted with the compliment and didn't want to let Robin down. I hope she doesn't make anything up, thought Hamish.

"Let me see, we go to bed at ten o'clock, and the bedroom's at the back. I got up about midnight to go to the, er, you know what. I took a wee keek out of the window there. I thought I heard a cry, but, och, it was probably a seagull."

"Nothing else?" asked Robin.

She shook her grey head.

"What about your sister? Did she see or hear anything?"

"No, Jessie's a heavy sleeper."

They thanked her and left. They were just walking away when Nessie called, "Detective Mackenzie!"

Robin hurried back. Nessie seized her arm and said in a fierce whisper, "You be careful of Macbeth. He's a devil with the women."

"What was that all about?" asked Hamish.

186

"A warning," said Robin. "She said you were a devil with the women."

Hamish sighed. "If only that were true. Let's go to the newspaper office and see if Matthew Campbell has found anything."

Elspeth was sitting at Matthew's desk. "Where's Matthew?" asked Hamish.

"Probably up at the hotel bar drinking with the other journalists."

"I am Detective Mackenzie," said Robin.

"Sorry," said Hamish. "Robin, this is Elspeth Grant, who used to work up here. She now works for the *Bugle* in Glasgow. Found anything out, Elspeth?"

"Not much. All the interesting characters at the hotel have been interviewed so many times they don't want to talk to me. I'm going out to talk to people in the village. You know, they'll talk to me where they might not talk to you, Hamish."

"Why?"

"I was the astrologer here, remember? They'll tell me things in the hope of getting their fortunes told. Like we said, I'll drop by the station tonight."

At the end of a long day, Hamish and Robin reported to the mobile police unit. Jimmy was asleep at the desk, an empty whisky glass in front of him. "He should never be in charge," said Robin. "Mr. Daviot should be here."

"He's all right," said Hamish defiantly. "The poor man's barely been able to have a sleep since Hal's body was found."

At the sound of their voices, Jimmy awoke. "Oh, it's you pair," he said. "Get anything?"

"Round and round the houses and nothing much," said Hamish. "Any more on the forensic report?"

"Just that he was struck dead further up the beach."

"Wait a bit," said Hamish. "That's odd."

"What's odd?"

"He was lying half in, half out of the water, faceup. Someone must have hit him and he fell backwards. So they'd drag the body down to the water by the ankles, hoping to dump him in the loch. Probably the murderer heard the boys coming and fled. Did forensic find any drag marks?"

Jimmy groaned. "They've got a rugby match tonight and cleared off fast. It's been high tide since then."

"You know, Jimmy, I watch these forensic programmes on TV. Whether fiction or fact, the labs always seem to have attractive, hardworking women. Why are we stuck with a lot of boozy men?"

"They're all staunch members of the Freemasons, and so is Daviot."

"Why couldn't that lot have joined some club or cult that bans liquor? So we can assume that whoever Hal met, it was someone he knew and someone he had no reason to fear. Maybe a woman."

"Maybe Jock. Maybe that wee notebook of Hal's contained something about Jock. That's it for the day. We'll start again tomorrow."

"Has Daviot been around?"

"He came briefly and fussed and hummed and hawed and then took himself off again."

Outside the unit, Robin said she would go back to Strathbane and get an early night.

Hamish fed and walked the dog and cat and was just wondering what to eat himself when Betty Barnard walked in.

"Unless it's police business," said Hamish sharply, "I shouldn't be talking to you."

"It is in a way. I know you've found out about Jock's previous charges of assault. I wanted to talk to you about him."

"So talk."

"Look, Hamish, why don't I drive us to that French restaurant in Strathbane for dinner and I can fill you in? Come on. It is police business we're discussing."

"I shouldn't be doing this," said Hamish, "but, och, why not? Who's to know?"

Betty talked on the road about how Dora had tricked Jock into marriage and how she had become paranoiac, believing Jock had an affair, all of which, Hamish thought uneasily, he knew already.

"I know it looks bad for Jock, but he's not really a violent man. The provocation in both cases was great."

Hamish suddenly remembered he had promised to talk to Elspeth. He took out his mobile and dialled the hotel, only to be told by Priscilla she had already left. "Tell her I've been called out on police duty," said Hamish.

"What was that about?" asked Betty.

"I was supposed to see Elspeth this evening, and I forgot."

"Poor Hamish. Us ladies won't stop chasing you."

He glanced sideways at her as she competently negotiated the one-track roads. Did she fancy him? She was so warm and easy-going and undemanding. He could be happy with her. But would she be happy being married to a highland policeman? Maybe, but only if he relocated to Glasgow.

She drove into Strathbane and headed for the docks. "It still looks the usual smelly run-down place it's always been," commented Hamish.

"It's all due for regeneration, and the owner of the restaurant decided to get in first while property is still at rock-bottom prices."

"Is he French?"

"He calls himself Pierre Lachasse."

Hamish looked amused. "As I recall, that's a famous cemetery in Paris."

"I thought there was something familiar about it. Here we are."

The restaurant was called Highland France. Inside, it was tastefully done up with wood panelling, plants, and curtains on brass rails. The maître d' took them to their table and handed them enormous menus.

"Stick to the set menu," said Betty. "I'm not being cheap, but it's every bit as good as anything on the à la carte."

They ordered snails to start and then salmon in a fennel sauce.

Hamish had never had snails before. He thought they were quite tasty, although a bit like garlic rubber.

He looked around the restaurant and then suddenly stiffened. "Well, I neffer did," he gasped.

"What?"

"Don't look now, but the boss, Peter Daviot, has just come in with Detective Mackenzie."

"What's odd about that?"

"I don't know what Mrs. Daviot would have to say about it. Oh, good, they've been put at a table where they can't see us."

What on earth was Daviot up to? wondered Hamish. And Robin? She was wearing a little black dress cut low enough to expose the tops of two excellent breasts. Her hair had just been done and rioted in curls around her well-made-up face.

"We're going to have a long meal," said Hamish. "I want to wait until they leave."

Betty grinned. "Suits me. Tell me more about the case."

But Hamish would not be drawn. Although he felt in his heart it was ridiculous, Betty was on the list of suspects. So he talked of old cases, spinning out the meal until he saw Daviot and Robin leave. He gloomily noticed that Daviot's face was lit up, and as he helped Robin on with her coat, he gazed down at her with adoring eyes.

The ambitious little minx, thought Hamish. I don't believe she cares for him one little bit.

He was tired and slept on the way home, only wakening when Betty drew up outside the police station. Betty leaned forward and planted a warm kiss on his cheek. "If only this wretched murder business were over, Hamish. Then we could really see more of each other."

Hamish went into the police station, his heart singing, until he saw a note on the kitchen table in Elspeth's handwriting. It simply said, "Bastard."

"I don't want any more women in my life at the moment," said Hamish as the dog and cat followed him into the bedroom. "I've enough on my plate."

But little did he know, there was going to be one more.

CHAPTER NINE

How happy could I be with either,
Were t'other dear charmer away!
— John Gay

"You've lost that look," complained Jock, working busily on Priscilla's portrait.

"What look?" asked Priscilla.

"The distant one, the remote one. What are you thinking about?"

"Nothing in particular."

"Didn't look that way," grumbled Jock.

Priscilla had been thinking about Hamish Macbeth. In London, it had been easy to dismiss him from her mind. But up here when he seemed to be pursued by other women, it was hard *not* to think about him.

Elspeth had confided in her that she had had an affair with Hamish and that she had presented him with an ultimatum — marriage or nothing else. Priscilla had been amazed at the bitter jealousy that admission had caused her. Now there was Betty Barnard.

Jock interrupted her thoughts again. "When I've finished this," he said tentatively, "would you consider buying it?"

"I'll think about it," said Priscilla. So even this artist hasn't got any designs on me other than money, she thought. Hamish has nothing to worry about.

Hamish was roused from his breakfast chores by a knock at the door. He assumed it was Robin and was wondering whether to say anything about having seen her last night. But then he would have to confess that he had been in the restaurant with Betty, and she would give him a stern lecture on socialising with a suspect.

But it was a strange woman who stood on the doorstep. "I am Mrs. Addenfest," she said.

"Come in," said Hamish, standing aside. She walked past him into the kitchen, a subtle perfume wafting about her.

She sat down at the kitchen table and crossed a pair of excellent legs. Her hair was an expensive dyed blonde — no brass, but a sort of silvery gold. She had high cheekbones, a full mouth, a straight little nose, and calculating brown eyes which betrayed

195

that she was actually much older than she looked. Hamish guessed she had gone in for an expensive facelift to match the expensive hair. She was dressed in Fifth Avenue's idea of suitable fashion for the Highlands of Scotland: a tweed jacket with patches at the elbows and a brown velvet collar and matching tweed skirt, sheer stockings, and brogues the colour of chestnuts.

"How can I help you?" he asked.

"I axed up at the hotel and was told you was the brightest around." The Brooklyn voice emanating from this richly manufactured beauty came as a surprise.

"So what is it you want from me?"

"Who killed him?"

"I wish I knew," said Hamish. "We're working hard on it. When did you arrive?"

"Last night. Fact is I feel I owe it to Hal — I mean, to be here and arrange the funeral and all. He never got around to changing his will, although he meant to leave me with zilch. I'm one rich lady."

"Coffee? Although I wouldnae recommend it. Tea's better."

"Tea's fine." She watched as Hamish put an old smoke-blackened kettle on the stove. She gave a harsh laugh. "You find out who murdered Hal and I'll buy you a new teakettle."

"There will be no need for that," said Hamish huffily. "I haff an electric one somewhere."

The cat and dog wandered in. She eyed the cat warily. "That looks like a lynx."

"It's a highland wild cat, but a domesticated one."

"Can you get rid of it for now? It scares the pants off me."

Hamish opened the kitchen door, and the dog and cat slouched out.

"Tell me about Hal," said Hamish. "How did you meet?"

"It was back in New York when I was working as a model. Hal was the type of man who liked arm candy. I was tired of slaving as a model, and with models getting younger and younger, I wanted security. He was working for an accounting firm and climbing fast up the corporate ladder. We rubbed along pretty well."

"I gather he divorced you and got out of paying anything."

"He could afford the best lawyers, and I couldn't. He'd put a private detective on me and found out I was having affairs. Jeez, he must be turning in his grave at the thought of me getting all his money. I'll give him a big send-off."

"Did he have any enemies?"

"Not murderous ones. Nobody liked him, but because he was chairman of the company, they all crawled to him. When he retired, though, he found no one wanted to know him. He was so vain he decided it must be my fault. I think he thought that if he got rid of me, he'd get friends. Didn't happen."

"Did you hear from him after he moved here?"

"Just one odd phone call. He said, 'Listen, you old bitch, I'm going to get married again and to a real woman who appreciates me and who doesn't go dropping her panties in motels for every trucker who takes her fancy.' I hung up on him, and that's the last I heard until you police got in touch with me. I went straight to his lawyers before I left, and bingo, Gloria's hit the jackpot."

"Gloria being you?"

"Sure. May I call you Hamish?"

"Of course."

"Okay, Hamish. Who's this female who's getting her portrait painted by Jock Fleming? Is she a suspect?"

"Priscilla Halburton-Smythe," said Hamish stiffly. "Her parents own the hotel. I've known her for a long time. Mrs. Addenfest, I would suggest strongly that

198

you leave all investigation to the police. There is a dangerous murderer out there."

"Look, I couldn't stand the man, but I've got his money and I feel, well, kinda responsible for him now. When's the coroner releasing the body?"

"We don't have coroners in Scotland. You need to contact the procurator fiscal's office. Hang on and I'll get you the address."

He went through to his office. When he came back, it was to find that Robin had arrived.

She was once more her neat and businesslike self. "Mrs. Addenfest and I are becoming acquainted," said Robin.

"How long will you be staying?" Hamish asked Gloria.

"Just till I get him buried."

"Aren't you taking the body back to the States?"

"Too much trouble. I'll see the preacher here and arrange a funeral. I've heard the Church of Scotland will bury anybody. He didn't have any religion. Like, he thought *he* was God." She picked up her handbag. "Where do I find the local preacher?"

"If you walk out to the waterfront and turn right, you'll see the church and the manse where he lives right next door."

"Thanks. See ya."

She departed on a cloud of perfume.

"What do you make of her?" asked Robin.

"Not much. She married for money, and I haff no time for the women who court men for money or for advancement in their jobs."

He looked narrowly at Robin. "You've got a love bite on your neck," he accused.

"I do have a private life, Hamish, and it has nothing to do with you."

Good God, thought Hamish, trying — and failing — to imagine Daviot in the throes of passion. What on earth was his boss doing? Daviot had always seemed like a rather rigid, moral man, given to preaching the benefits of family life.

"Stop staring at me!" snapped Robin.

"I was thinking about the ex-wife. I wonder when she arrived. It would be really difficult if it turns out we have two murderers. We'll go and see Jimmy and find out if he checked when she arrived in this country."

Priscilla made her way up to Jock's temporary studio for the morning session. There was no sign of Jock. She waited and waited, but he did not arrive. Priscilla had told Jock that she would need to consider

200

if she had enough money to pay for the portrait. Jock had said she could have it for the "knock-down price" of ten thousand pounds.

At last, she rose and lifted the cover off the painting to see how he was getting on. She let out a cry of dismay. It looked as if someone had taken a rag soaked in turpentine and smeared it right across the portrait to obliterate the face.

Priscilla ran downstairs and phoned Hamish on his mobile.

Hamish arrived with Robin, and they went up to the studio. "I'll need to get this whole room dusted for fingerprints," said Hamish. "Lock it up."

He phoned Jimmy and explained what had happened. After Priscilla had locked the studio, he said he would need to ask Betty Barnard, Mrs. Addenfest, and Jock himself for permission to search their rooms.

Betty looked mildly hurt. "Now, why would I go about destroying my client's work, Hamish?"

"It's just a process of elimination," said Hamish.

Betty's room was a mess, with clothes lying on the bed and scattered on the floor.

"I can never decide what to wear," said Betty defensively. There seemed to be nothing incriminating, but Hamish had not expected there would be. He had suggested searching Betty's room because he did not want to be accused of favouritism. Mrs. Addenfest was nowhere in the hotel. Hamish assumed she was at the manse talking to the minister.

Jock was nowhere to be found. They searched the hotel and the grounds. Hamish borrowed a pair of binoculars and went out to the car park and focussed them up towards the mountains. Then he made out a figure up at Geordie's Cleft. He adjusted the focus to get a sharper image. It was Jock, sitting at an easel.

"He's up at Geordie's Cleft," said Hamish. "We'd better get up there."

Robin looked down ruefully at her neat court shoes. "I'm not exactly dressed for climbing."

"You wait here for the forensic people," said Hamish. "I'll go."

It was one of those white summer days in the Highlands when the sky is covered by a thin veil of cloud and all colour seems to have been bleached out of the landscape. The air was warm and humid, and the midges, those Scottish mosquitoes, were out in force. Hamish liberally applied repellent to his face and neck from a stick he always kept in his pocket. He drove up as far as he could and then got out and began to walk, his large regulation boots occasionally slipping on the scree.

He met Jock as the artist was on his way down. "Waste of time, Hamish," shouted Jock as he approached the policeman. "The weather just turned, and there doesn't seem to be a bit of colour anywhere. You're obviously looking for me. Why?"

"Someone has defaced that portrait of Priscilla."

"What!"

"Someone has taken turpentine and scrubbed the face out."

"I'll kill the bastard who did this," raged Jock. "I'll get compensation from that hotel."

"Won't work," said Hamish. "They've given you a free room and a studio. They're not responsible for protecting your work. You didn't lock up the studio, did you?"

"Didn't see the need," said Jock bitterly. "I'm getting out of this hellish place."

"I want you to stay here a bit longer."

They both began to slither down the hill. "It's a bit insensitive of you to be up at Geordie's Cleft."

"Why? It gives the best panoramic view, and Effie was nothing to me."

"When did you last do any work on the portrait?"

"Yesterday afternoon."

"And you haven't been inside the studio since?"

"I went in early this morning, around eight, to pick up my paints. I had a look at the portrait. It was all right then."

"Do the maids clean the studio?"

"No, they've got orders to leave it alone until I'm finished. I suppose there's no use going on with it now. Oh, man, what a waste!"

I must get more on Jock's background, thought Hamish. I wonder if his money goes to something like drugs or gambling. Aloud, he said, "Hal's ex-wife has arrived."

"What's she like?"

"Very rich now. Hal never got round to changing his will."

"Might have a crack at her. Wouldn't mind having enough to travel the world without this pressure of producing canvas after canvas."

"Surely you've got enough money now."

"I spend a lot, and then Dora takes a chunk for the kids' welfare."

They had reached Hamish's Land Rover. "You go on down to the police unit and report," said Hamish. "I'm going to see Effie's sister."

Caro invited Hamish in. She had been working at a small easel. "I hope there have been no more murders," she said.

"No, but Jock's painting of Priscilla has been defaced."

"But that's dreadful. How? When?"

"He saw it at eight o'clock this morning, so it must have been shortly after that. Where were you?"

"Why should I . . . ? Oh, for heaven's sake. I was here."

"Anyone see you?"

"Up here? No, not a soul. Why on earth should I deface one of Jock's paintings?"

"Because maybe you suspect him of the murder of your sister."

"That's ridiculous."

"Is it? You must wonder who did it."

"I don't, and do you know why? I think Effie committed suicide. She could have had that note and wine bottle ready and put it on the doorstep when I turned away to get in my car. She was always jealous of

205

me. I think Jock's rejection of her and the shame of having been found out as a liar by the whole village must have turned her mind."

"And you're convinced of this?"

"Absolutely."

When Hamish left her cottage, he felt the bonnet of her car. It was warm. He turned back and looked thoughtfully at the cottage. Caro's white face glimmered back at him through the small window. But the day was unusually warm. That might explain it.

Hamish parked the Land Rover on the waterfront and was going to the police unit when he was accosted by Elspeth.

"So what's your explanation for last night?" she demanded.

"Elspeth, I'm right sorry. I forgot."

"You were seen driving off with Betty Barnard."

"Oh, all *right,* Elspeth. But I don't need to explain my movements to you."

She studied him thoughtfully and then said, "Do you know what your problem is? You're afraid of love. You'd rather settle for companionship. Does Betty know she's got serious competition?"

"Like who?"

"Like your cat and your dog. You know

206

what you are? You're nothing more than an old maid."

"Get the hell away from me," raged Hamish, his highland vanity cut to the quick. Then he gave a malicious smile. "So don't you think there's something up with you, hanging around and nagging someone who doesn't want you?"

Elspeth slapped him full across the face and walked off.

Hamish became aware of the curious eyes of villagers. He glared back and went into the police unit to be told that Mr. Daviot had arrived and was up at the castle with Robin and Jimmy.

He decided to go back to the police station and take Sonsie and Lugs for a walk so he could think in peace. "And if there's some woman waiting for me," he muttered, "I'll strangle her."

But he could hardly strangle his boss's wife.

With a sinking heart, he recognised the matronly figure of Mrs. Daviot waiting for him on the doorstep.

He had always considered the Daviots the very picture of a contented marriage. Mr. Daviot with his sleek grey hair, impeccably tailored suits, and smoothly shaven cheeks looked more like a successful businessman than a police superintendent. Mrs. Daviot was small and trim with dyed-brown hair in neat, permed curls and large blue eyes in a carefully made-up face.

"Come in, Mrs. Daviot," said Hamish. "Are you looking for your husband?"

"No, I'm looking for you." Her voice trembled on the edge of tears.

Oh, dear, thought Hamish. She suspects something.

"Would you like some tea?"

"No, yes . . . well, maybe."

"I'll take that as a yes. How can I help you?"

She sat down at the table and clasped her handbag on her lap. "I think Peter is having an affair."

"What makes you think that?"

"He says he's going out to some police function or other, and then I find out there was no such function. He smells of perfume. He looks excited, elated. He mutters into the phone, and if I walk into the room, he hangs up."

"It could all just be police business, after all," said Hamish awkwardly. He poured tea and told her to help herself to milk and sugar.

"I want you to investigate. I want you to find out who she is."

"It's right difficult," said Hamish. "He is my boss. I think he'd fire me like a shot if he even guessed what I was doing."

"Please, Hamish." Her eyes swam with tears. "I'm begging you."

He sighed. "I'll do my best."

She opened her handbag and took out a card case. "Here's my mobile phone number. Phone me night or day if you find out anything."

"What will you do if it turns out to be true?"

"I'll divorce him."

"That's a wee bit extreme. If there is something, it could just be a passing fancy."

"My husband," she said grimly, "is not allowed passing fancies."

After Mrs. Daviot had left, Hamish went out towards the police unit. Back from the Tommel Castle, Superintendent Daviot was standing outside, smoking a cigarette.

"Sir," said Hamish.

"Ah, good morning. Isn't it a glorious morning, Hamish?"

"Yes, indeed, sir."

"We must get these murders solved. I'm giving a press conference up at the hotel this evening. The press are becoming very strident."

"Maybe some other big story will happen to take them away," said Hamish. "They're really more interested in political scandal than anything else these days. Do you remember that foreign minister last year who was found to be having an affair with a researcher? What a carry-on that was, and for once, the wife didn't stand by him but demanded a divorce. It was the end o' his career. You know, sir, I often wonder what makes important men throw their careers away all because of a fling."

"Maybe he was deeply in love with her," said Daviot, staring at Hamish.

"Not if you remember the aftermath. Because he was out of a job, he suddenly looked at her and wondered what he had ever seen in her. Of course, if he'd been philandering up here in the Highlands, everyone would have known about it from the word go. Everyone knows everyone else's business up here."

"Except when it comes to witnessing a murder," said Daviot.

"Now, that's what's so odd," said Hamish. "Normally you can't even take a walk across the moors without someone having seen you. I can only conclude the murderer was extremely lucky. Has Detective Mackenzie arrived?"

"Yes, she's inside the unit. What do you think of her?"

"I think she is keen and ambitious. She'll rise right to the top. Only trouble is she might not be too nice about how she gets there." Hamish touched his cap. "I'll just go inside and get my briefing. Give my best to your good wife, sir. Splendid woman."

After the door of the unit had closed behind Hamish, Daviot stood for a long moment before angrily crushing out his cigarette. He was damn sure Hamish Macbeth had just given him a warning.

But his obsession for Robin gripped hard. He started guiltily when the door of the unit opened and she came out.

"Peter, darling," she whispered. "A word with you."

"What is it?"

"This press conference this evening. I was thinking the press can be very aggressive. I thought it might be a good idea if I fielded the questions for you."

For the first time, Daviot wondered whether she was using him. The television cameras would be there. She was really too low in rank to even suggest such a thing.

"No, I do not think that's a good idea at all. I am surprised you should even suggest such a thing. Please go back to your duties and remember to call me 'sir.' We are, after all, in the middle of a murder investigation."

"But Peter . . ."

"Detective Mackenzie, please remember our relative positions."

"Like the missionary one?" snapped Robin.

He took a deep breath. "I have made a bad mistake. Either get a transfer or get on with your work here. I do not want to see you outside work again."

"Hamish!" shouted Jimmy. "I've been trying to talk to you, and you've been glued to that window."

"Sorry," said Hamish, turning round.

"I want you to go and see Jock's ex-wife again. I find it odd the way she's hanging around."

Robin came into the unit. Her face was red, and her eyes were angry.

"Take Detective Mackenzie with you," said Jimmy.

Robin and Hamish walked in silence along to Sea View. Mrs. Dunne said Dora Fleming had left earlier, saying she was going up to the hotel to see Jock.

"We'll take the Land Rover," said

Hamish. "It's almost as if our Dora had something on Jock."

They found Dora and Jock at a corner table in the bar. They were holding hands and talking urgently, their heads together.

They broke off when they saw Hamish and Robin. "What now?" asked Jock truculently.

"I really wanted to talk to Mrs. Fleming here," said Hamish.

Jock rose to his feet. "Right. I'm off."

They waited until he had left and sat down opposite Dora. Dora was picking a beer mat apart with long red nails. Prostitutes are always terrible fidgets, thought Hamish.

Hamish looked at Robin, but she seemed lost in her own thoughts, so he began the questioning.

"I was wondering, Mrs. Fleming, why you're still in Lochdubh. You must miss your children."

"I was telt not to leave, and the children are just fine with my mither."

"You and Jock appear to have patched up any differences."

"What's that to you?"

"Did you know that Hal Addenfest, the dead man, took notes of what everyone was saying?"

"No."

"I find it hard to believe that you didn't. Everyone in Lochdubh knew about it."

"They don't talk to me."

"Come on. Mrs. Dunne gossips to everyone. I can ask her."

"She may have said something. Wasnae important anyway. Nothing that goes on in this arsehole of the world is important."

"I tell you what I'll do for you," said Hamish. "I'll have a word with my boss and get you permission to leave."

"I'll leave when I'm good and ready."

When they left her, Hamish saw Priscilla and Betty talking in the reception area. Betty gave him a wink and a cheeky smile. Priscilla's face was smooth and expressionless.

"Where now?" asked Robin, jerking herself out of her thoughts with an effort.

"Back to Sea View. I wonder if Mrs. Dunne heard anything."

"As far as I remember from the reports, she said she hadn't."

"Nonetheless, I would like to try again. I wonder if Dora Fleming was in her bed all night."

Mrs. Dunne complained she was too busy to answer any more questions. "That's a pity," said Robin, and then

214

trotted out her usual compliment. "You see, people often do hear or see something and only remember it later. And you, being such an obviously quick-witted and intelligent lady, might just have remembered something."

"What we're after," put in Hamish, "is whether you are sure that Dora Fleming spent all night in her bed."

Mrs. Dunne stood frowning. She had been flattered by Robin's compliment. "There was one thing," she said slowly. "I thought I heard a wee noise at the back of the house."

"Like what?"

"A sort of bang. I've got Mrs. Fleming here and a couple from Glasgow and three of the forestry workers. They were all in their rooms when I locked up. Och, I mind the days when I wouldn't have bothered, but it's a wicked world now."

"Don't the guests have their own keys?"

"I don't trust anyone with the keys. I wait until they're all indoors."

"So how would anyone get out?"

"There's the fire door at the back on the first."

"Show it to us."

She led the way upstairs and along a corridor on the first landing. Hamish studied the fire door, and then his sharp eyes noticed a small square wad of paper lying on the floor. He took out a pair of tweezers, lifted the paper, and put it in a cellophane envelope.

He thanked Mrs. Dunne and went back outside the building, followed by Robin.

"Why did you pick up that paper?" asked Robin.

"It could have been used to wedge the door so that someone could get back in again. Let's get back to the unit and examine it properly."

He explained to Jimmy what he had found. Then he took out the envelope and, putting on gloves, extracted the wad of paper. He laid it on Jimmy's desk and gently opened it up. "It's out o' a film magazine," Hamish said. "See, there's a bit from the top of the page — *Hollywood World*. I'll go over to Patel's and see if he sold a copy to anyone." Robin went with him.

Mr. Patel said he only ordered two copies a month, the locals being more interested in magazines that dealt with television soaps than anything to do with the movies.

"Who bought them?"

"Mrs. Wellington bought one." Hamish

blinked in amazement. He'd never have guessed that the tweedy minister's wife would want to read about movie stars.

"And the other one?"

"Oh, it was that wee woman who was married to the artist."

They hurried back to tell Jimmy. "Good work," he said. "Bring her in."

They found Dora Fleming crossing the humpback bridge on her way to the boarding house. They marched her back to the police unit and took her inside.

"What's this all about?" she demanded.

"This," said Jimmy, pointing to the piece from the film magazine. "This was lying by the fire door at Sea View. We think you used it to wedge the fire door when you crept out so you'd be able to get back in again."

"Don't be daft. It's just a piece of paper."

"It's from a film magazine which you bought. The paper's glossy, and we should get your prints off it. In fact, we'll finger-print you now."

"I want a lawyer," she screeched.

"You've already got her fingerprints," interposed Robin. "We took the fingerprints of everyone who might be concerned right after Mr. Addenfest's murder."

"So we did," said Jimmy with his foxy grin. "Right, young woman, where did you go, when, and why?"

"I didnae go anywhere!"

"We'll look at the steps down from the fire door," said Jimmy. "I'm sure we'll find some footprints."

She stared at him in mulish silence.

"Right," said Jimmy. "I am taking you into police headquarters for questioning. Hamish, you and Robin go back to Sea View and have a look at the steps down from the fire door. See if you can find anything."

As two policemen escorted Dora out to the car which was to take her to Strathbane, Jimmy phoned Daviot, who was up at the hotel arranging a room for the press conference. He told him of Hamish's find. "It was a right smart piece of work on Macbeth's part," said Jimmy. "You can at least tell the press we've got a suspect."

Mrs. Dunne took Hamish and Robin round to the back of the house where an iron staircase led down from the fire door. "We'd better not add our own footprints," said Hamish. The stairs led down to a weedy back garden. "We'll just need to search through the garden and see if we can find anything."

He knelt down and began to feel his way through the rough grass with his fingers. Robin was wearing a skirt and did not want to ladder her tights by following Hamish's example.

"I've got to go to the loo," she called. "Be back soon."

She went round to the front of the house, knocked, and asked Mrs. Dunne if she could use her bathroom.

"Don't leave a mess," said Mrs. Dunne. "I keep a clean house."

Robin carefully reapplied her make-up. Daviot's rejection of her request to be at the press conference rankled, and she knew she would feel more confident if she brushed her hair and made up her face.

When she went out again, she saw Daviot's car heading along the waterfront and eagerly flagged him down.

Daviot lowered the window. "What is it, Detective Mackenzie?"

"I had a marvellous piece of luck," said Robin. "I found a piece of a magazine by the fire door at Sea View which had been used to wedge the door. I found out Dora Fleming had bought that magazine and —"

He interrupted her, his voice cold and measured. "I have already heard of Hamish Macbeth's detective work. Do not try to take credit from another officer again."

The car window rolled up in her face, he tapped his driver on the shoulder, and the car moved on.

Robin felt miserable. She had dreamt of taking over Blair's job one day. She trailed back to the garden to find Hamish putting something into an envelope.

"What have you found?" she asked.

"A used condom."

"So what's special about that? The local lads probably use this garden for a bit of nooky."

"No, they don't," said Hamish. "I'll take this straight over to Strathbane. Are you coming?"

But Robin did not want to run into Daviot.

CHAPTER TEN

O what a tangled web we weave,
When first we practise to deceive!
— Sir Walter Scott

Hamish did not have any hope of a speedy DNA analysis of the used condom, but for once, Daviot was really desperate for answers. Forensic swabs were taken from Jock and the men living in the boarding house and sent to the forensic laboratory in Aberdeen along with the condom.

While he waited for the results, the investigation seemed to have temporarily ground to a halt. Mrs. Daviot phoned him in high excitement to say that her husband, once the case was closed, was going to take her on a second honeymoon. Robin came into the police station just as Hamish was putting down the phone.

"That was Mrs. Daviot," said Hamish.

Robin eyed him warily. "If she's looking

for her husband, he's on his way from Strathbane."

"She just wanted to tell me that they are going on a second honeymoon once this case is over. Now, isn't that romantic?"

"Oh, sure," she said sarcastically. "I've got some news about Mrs. Addenfest."

"What's that?"

"She said she arrived at Glasgow airport after she had been notified of Hal's death. But she was in the country before Hal died. She arrived at London airport two days before his murder. I don't know how she hoped to conceal it. Checked with New York police, and they said they got the number of her cell phone — that's American for mobile — and called her on that with the news because she was out when they visited her flat and her maid gave them the number."

"He can't have left her that broke if she had a maid. Didn't the maid tell the police she had gone to Britain?"

"The maid has about two words of English. Mrs. Addenfest's over at the unit. I've come to fetch you."

They walked out together. "Men are bastards," said Robin, suddenly and viciously.

"You're talking to one."

She shrugged in reply.

Gloria Addenfest was seated before Jimmy in the unit. Her perfume hit them like a scented wall when they walked in.

Hamish felt a rush of gratitude for Jimmy. He was so used to Blair keeping him away from every interview.

"Now we're all here," said Jimmy, "you'd better explain why you lied to us about your arrival in this country."

"I thought it looked bad," said Gloria, crossing her long legs. "So I lied. No big deal. I didn't murder him."

"So when did you really arrive up here?"

"Right after the cops phoned me about him being murdered. I came straight up from London."

"What were you doing in London?"

"Look, it's like this, see." Gloria lit a cigarette. "I'll come clean. I really meant to come up here and confront the little rat. They had an audit at his company and found Hal had been embezzling. I remembered his high and mighty moral tone at the divorce proceedings, the way his lawyers made me look like a whore. I wanted to see his face when I told him his firm's lawyers had been to the police and were trying to get an extradition order. I just wanted to see the look on his stupid face.

But I stayed in London."

"Why?"

"Do I have to tell you?"

Hamish regarded her with amusement. "You met someone on the plane over," he said.

She flushed angrily. "Well, okay. He was in pharmaceuticals, and we hit it off. He said he'd show me a good time. We moved into the Ritz together and started to do the town."

"Name?" asked Jimmy.

"Must I? He's married."

"Name!"

"James Roden. He's still at the Ritz as far as I know."

"We'll check out your alibi. In the meantime, stay in Lochdubh and give us your passport. Now, how much had Mr. Addenfest embezzled?"

"Close to a million. He'd been siphoning it off over the years. Funny, though," said Gloria. "He had one hell of a salary. But he was secretive and nasty. He probably enjoyed ripping them off."

Jimmy got a statement typed up and told her to sign it, then got a police officer to escort her back to the hotel.

"There are too many women in this case, and all of them seem to be covering up for something," said Jimmy. "The forensic lab promised us the DNA results fast. Meanwhile, keep asking around the village if anyone saw anything. I know you've done it over and over again, but folks are funny. Sometimes they come out with something amazing that they never even thought of telling us at the time."

"Who first?" asked Robin outside.

"I've got a salmon in the freezer."

"So what?"

"So we'll go back and see Angus."

The seer invited Hamish in but grumbled that the salmon was frozen, saying he liked it fresh-caught.

"Have you thought of anything, Angus?" asked Hamish.

The seer leaned back in his chair and closed his eyes. "Women everywhere," he said. "Manipulating women." He opened his eyes and looked at Robin. "You were out to ruin a marriage. Just thank the stars you didnae succeed."

"Forget about Detective Mackenzie," said Hamish impatiently. "I know all about that."

Robin's face flamed.

Angus settled back in his chair again and closed his eyes. If the old sod goes to sleep this time, I'll strike him, thought Hamish. I want one salmon's worth.

"Strong sexual urges and bad, bad jealousy," crooned Angus. "You're looking for a woman."

"Which woman?"

Angus opened his eyes. "The spirits have left me."

"I expected more for a whole fish," exclaimed Hamish.

"So who *have* we got?" asked Hamish as he and Robin walked down to the police Land Rover. "We've got Caro Garrard, Gloria Addenfest, Dora Fleming, and Betty Barnard."

"My money's on Dora," said Robin.

"I thought you suspected Betty."

"I think it's Dora now. She's had a rough, coarse life. I bet she was in a lot of fights when she was on the streets."

"But what would Dora have to do with the murder of Effie?"

"Maybe Effie's death *was* suicide."

"Hal phoned his wife to say he was getting married," said Hamish. "One of the women must have been seen with him. We'd better go up to the hotel and start again."

"All that stuff about me trying to break

up someone's marriage was rubbish," said Robin. "You said you knew."

"I don't think you planned to break up a marriage, more to sleep your way to the top."

Hamish's phone rang before Robin had time to reply. "Get back here immediately," Jimmy ordered. "They've phoned over the DNA results."

"Whose is it?" demanded Hamish as soon as he and Robin walked into the police unit.

"Jock Fleming. They've gone to fetch him," said Jimmy.

"Where's Mrs. Fleming?"

"We had to let her go for the moment. That night, she says, she wanted to go down to the garden at the back for a bit of fresh air. She said if she'd gone out the front, the sound of all the locks being unlocked would have woken Mrs. Dunne. Mind you, I've sent some men to go through that room of hers again, looking for the least little thing. That sounds like Jock arriving now."

The artist was brought in. He looked at them wearily. "What now?"

"Sit down," barked Jimmy.

Jock slumped down in the chair in front of him.

"A used condom was found in the back garden at Sea View. We found your DNA on it. Now your ex-wife says that on the night Addenfest was murdered, she went out through the fire door and down into the back garden for a bit of air."

"It's all very simple," said Jock. "She wanted to talk about more money. One thing led to another. We had a quickie up against the garden wall."

A policeman who had just walked in interrupted them. "Sir," he said to Jimmy, "sorry to interrupt, but this was found stitched into the hem of the curtains." He held out a glassine envelope full of white powder. "I tested a bit. It's cocaine."

"Get Dora Fleming along here."

Jimmy glared at Jock. "Do you know what I think? I think you wanted that notebook of Addenfest's because you were frightened that there was something in there that would incriminate you. I think you miserable pair — you and your ex-wife — got high. I think one of you lured him to the beach, and you both killed him to cover up the murder of Effie Garrard."

"This is rubbish," blustered Jock.

"And why should you want sex with a wife you divorced?"

"She's got certain interesting tricks."

228

I am slipping, thought Hamish ruefully. I had thought he was such a nice ordinary man.

Dora was brought in. Jimmy waved the envelope of cocaine in front of her. "This was found sewn into the curtains of your room."

"That's naethin' tae dae wi' me!" she shrieked. "You lot must ha' planted it there."

"Enough of this," said Jimmy. He turned to his waiting police officers. "Take them over to police headquarters. I'll interview them separately."

As they were led out, volubly protesting, Hamish said, "That's odd."

"I'm off," said Jimmy. "What's odd?"

"Dora Fleming shows no sign of being a drug user. Someone *could* have planted those drugs."

"Why?"

"To muddy the waters."

"Go back to Mrs. Fleming's room and see if you can see anything that might have been missed."

Robin felt uneasily that as the superior officer she should be taking the initiative, not Hamish. But Daviot's rejection had thrown her, and she was sure he would do everything in his power to block any promotion. She wished these murder cases would get solved quickly now so that she could put in for a transfer.

Mrs. Dunne was furious. She followed them up the stairs to Dora's room protesting that she kept a decent house and somehow it was all Hamish's fault. Hamish and Robin went into Dora's room, and Hamish shut the door firmly in Mrs. Dunne's angry face.

There was a sour smell in the room. "She doesn't believe in washing much," said Robin, wrinkling her nose, "and her dirty clothes are lying everywhere."

"Let's see these curtains," said Hamish. He knelt down on the floor and studied the unpicked hem. The curtains were acid green and of a cheap synthetic material. They were short, and when he drew them closed, the light shone through them. "That's how they saw the envelope of drugs," he said. "They would look at the curtains and see it outlined against the light. And look. The stitches are very neat. I cannot imagine one such as Dora Fleming being a good needlewoman."

"So you think the drugs were planted?"

"Maybe. Let's have a good look around."

They searched the room thoroughly but

found nothing incriminating. "I tell you what," said Hamish. "Do you mind if I leave you alone for a bit? I've a personal call to make."

"And I've got someone to see in Strathbane," said Robin. She had decided to confront Daviot and see if she could use a bit of emotional blackmail on him.

"Right. I'll meet you back at the police unit at, say, three o'clock."

Hamish headed up to the hotel. He had a sudden longing to see Priscilla, to sit in her calm presence as he had done in the past and talk about the case.

He found her in the gift shop, selling a mohair sweater to a tourist. After she had finished, Hamish asked, "Any chance of a talk?"

"I'll just close up the shop and tell Mr. Johnson if anyone wants anything to tell them to come back later. You look worried."

She locked the shop door. "We'll use the gunroom."

"I hope it's kept securely locked," said Hamish uneasily.

"It's locked and burglar-alarmed."

Hamish waited while Priscilla unlocked the gun room door and reset the alarm.

They sat down in battered old leather chairs. A reflection of Priscilla's face swam in the glass of one of the cabinets, and dust motes danced in the shafts of sunlight coming in through the windows.

Hamish began to talk, going over everything he had learned.

He wound up by saying, "I fear there is something far wrong with Jock Fleming. What sort of man sneaks out at night to have sex with his ex-wife up against a garden wall?"

"It's a new one for you, Hamish. You see, I don't think you've come across someone so completely amoral as Jock Fleming before. It is my opinion he would screw the cat."

"Has he made a pass at you?"

"Not even a flicker. It's my money he's after. And there's a point: You say drugs were found? Maybe Jock's a drug addict."

"I don't believe it. Neither Jock nor Dora shows the slightest sign of drugs — unless you count alcohol as a drug. I think someone really did plant it there and someone very clever who knew that with the sun shining through those cheap curtains, the envelope would be spotted."

"So either someone knew about the fire door or someone managed to get in during the day unseen. How could they do that?"

"Mrs. Dunne doesn't lock the outside door during the day. It took a strong nerve to sneak in there and calmly sit sewing that envelope into the curtains. I'd better ask around again. Maybe someone saw someone going into Mrs. Dunne's who doesn't live there."

"There's something mad, calculating, and cunning about our murderer," said Priscilla. "And somehow, though Jock may not be the murderer, it's something to do with him. Unless, of course, Effie's sister is right and she really did commit suicide and Hal's wife knew about his will and decided to finish him off before he got married to whoever he was talking about."

"That's if there was another woman," said Hamish. "He could just have been saying that out of malice."

"And yet he went out in the middle of the night to meet someone."

"Could be someone from his past, someone we don't know about."

"What about Betty Barnard?"

"Hard to imagine," said Hamish stiffly. "Oh, well, I'd better get off and start questioning people. That means starting with the Currie sisters, since they're next door to Sea View."

Hamish started by questioning Nessie Currie, mentally editing out the Greek chorus that was her sister.

"I saw no one going in there that shouldnae be going in there," said Nessie. "There was just the folks that live there when I looked and the postie."

"What time of day did you see the postie?"

"Must have been about lunchtime yesterday."

"But the postman only delivers at nine in the morning."

"Then it must have been a special delivery because he walked right in."

"Did you see him come out?"

"I've got more to do with my day than stand on my doorstep and watch people."

"What did this postman look like?"

"Tall. One of thae baseball caps. Couldn't see his face."

It could have been easy for someone to masquerade as a postman, thought Hamish. Navy clothes, a canvas bag, and a baseball cap pulled well down. Must have known Dora Fleming wasn't due back for a while. So we're looking for a man. Maybe it's Jock, after all.

He thanked Nessie and went along the

waterfront, questioning one villager after another. A few had seen the postman. He had arrived on a bicycle, but they could not add anything further to Nessie's description of him.

Then Hamish remembered that the hotel had a few bicycles for use by more energetic guests.

He headed back to the hotel and asked the manager if he could take a look at the bikes.

"Go and take a look yourself," said Mr. Johnson. "They're in a shed by the kitchen door. It's not locked during the day. No one's taken one out for months."

Hamish went round to the back of the hotel. He could hear the clatter of dishes from the kitchen. He went to the shed and opened the door. There were six mountain bikes.

At first, they all seemed to be clean and oiled. The roads had been dusty. He went from one to the other. The one at the end had a thin film of dust on it. Need to get this fingerprinted, he thought. Things are looking bad for Jock.

He went back to the mobile unit to meet Robin. Her face was flushed, and she looked as if she had been crying.

Robin had gone to Strathbane to see

Daviot. He had received her coldly. Robin asked him what had happened between them, and he had said his affair with her had been nothing but a bit of dangerous folly and that he loved his wife.

Upset and furious, Robin tried to hint that she could make life difficult for him if the affair ever came to light.

"If you do that," Daviot had said, "I will deny everything. I should never have got mixed up with a harpy like you. I am arranging for you to be transferred to Inverness. You start there next week. My secretary will give you the details."

Robin knew she was beaten. If she did make the affair public, then she would be found to be the guilty one in the chauvinistic world of the police force.

She seemed barely to listen when Hamish told her about the bicycle and suggested they both go to Strathbane to interrupt Jimmy's interview.

"You go," she said. "I'll keep on asking questions."

Robin wandered along the waterfront. The air was close and warm, and midges stung at her cheeks and bare arms. She stopped to slap at them when she heard herself being hailed by Elspeth. "You should go to Patel's and get some repellent," said Elspeth. "In the meantime, have some of mine."

"Thanks." Robin took the stick from her and applied it.

"How's the case going?" asked Elspeth.

"Who cares?" said Robin bitterly. "I'm sick of the police. You know, I always thought policemen would be honourable, but they're just rats like any other men. Take you to bed one night and claim the moral high ground the next. Makes me sick."

She handed back the repellent and strode off, leaving Elspeth staring after her in dismay.

Faithless, philandering Hamish, thought Elspeth bitterly. She went back to the local newspaper office and phoned the news editor in Glasgow.

"Things have ground to a halt up here," she said.

"We could do with you back in Glasgow," said the editor. "But your colour pieces have been very good. What about a piece on that local copper? File it and then come back. We can always send you up again if anything breaks."

Elspeth switched on her laptop and began to write. Her fingers seemed to fly across the keyboard.

* * *

Hamish pulled Jimmy out of an interview to tell him about the postman and the hotel bicycle which looked as if it had been used.

"What are they playing at?" asked Jimmy, meaning Jock and his wife.

"I cannae see that either Jock or Dora would put those drugs in Dora's room. Why should they?"

"I'll get someone to check with the post office and see if there was any delivery made to Sea View that day. Get back to Lochdubh and see if you can find out more."

"Will you have to release them?"

"I'll need to release Jock when six hours are up, but I can hang on to Dora with a drugs charge."

"Get the medical examiner to look at both of them," said Hamish. "I'll bet anything you don't find a single bit of evidence of drugs."

"She could have been selling the stuff."

"Who to? It's mostly alcohol here and a bit of pot. Why come up here to sell drugs when she could be doing a roaring trade in Glasgow?"

"Anyway, go back and check. Meanwhile, the FBI are checking Hal's background. They'll let us know if he had any enemies."

Hamish did not immediately head back. He wanted to walk and think. There was something tugging at the back of his mind. He felt that if he could get to it, he might have an inkling about the identity of the murderer.

He wandered past shops and pubs, lost in thought.

The sky above was changing from grey to black. Thunder coming, thought Hamish. I hope it clears the air.

He realised he was hungry and went into a café and ordered a mutton pie and peas and washed it down with strong tea.

As he glanced out of the window, he saw Betty Barnard walking past. He half rose to his feet to go outside and hail her but then sank back down. He must not socialise with a suspect. Then he was suddenly curious to find out where she was going.

He paid for his food and went out. He could just see her at the end of the street, turning the corner, and hurried after her. She went into a small picture gallery which showed touristy scenes of hills and heather. He went up and looked quickly in the window. She was talking to someone in the gallery and looking at a painting.

Well, what else did I expect? thought Hamish. Something sinister?

He heard a low rumble of thunder in the distance and made his way back to police headquarters, where he had parked the Land Rover.

As he drove up into the hills, one fat raindrop slid down the windscreen to be followed by another. Then the heavens opened and the rain poured down. The thunder boomed and rolled round the mountains and glens, and jagged lightning jabbed down on the road ahead.

When he reached the police station, he rushed indoors and switched on the kitchen light. Nothing. A power cut.

He found an oil lamp, lit it, and put it on the kitchen table and began to prepare food for Sonsie and Lugs.

He realised he was very tired. After the animals had been fed, he put out the oil lamp and locked the kitchen door.

Hamish went through and lay on his back on his bed. Lugs climbed up and lay on his feet, and Sonsie stretched out beside him. Just a few minutes' peace and quiet, thought Hamish.

Hamish awoke with a start to find it was

early evening. The clouds had rolled away, and a shaft of the setting sun shone into his bedroom.

He rose and went outside to check there had been no storm damage to the out-buildings and then locked up his hens for the night.

Then he made his way along to the police unit, but it was closed and locked, and there was no sign of Robin. He walked round to see Matthew Campbell. The reporter answered his door in his shirt-sleeves.

"Come in, Hamish. Got a story for me?"

"I wish I had. All the press still around?"

"No, most of them have gone. It's yesterday's story. Besides, guess what: Someone's seen the Loch Ness Monster and claims to have a photograph."

"Convenient in the middle of the tourist season," said Hamish cynically. "Is Elspeth still around?"

"She wrote some colour piece that she wouldn't let me see and then cleared off to Glasgow."

Hamish felt a sharp pang of loss. He should have been nicer to her, but, then, she'd said some dreadful things to him.

"Are you still enjoying it up here?" asked Hamish.

"Yes, I do pretty well. The local job's not very demanding, but I make a good bit covering for the nationals."

"I'll tell you about the latest development," said Hamish, "and see what you think. But, mind, you didn't hear it from me."

"Okay."

Hamish told him about the postman, the drugs, and the questioning of Jock and Dora.

"Can I use this?" asked Matthew eagerly.

"I don't see why not. The locals have all been questioned, so you would have heard about this postman sooner or later. Help me. I'm tired of questioning and questioning. See if anyone can tell you anything more about this postman. All I've got is he was in dark clothes and wearing a baseball cap with the peak pulled down over his face."

"I'll get on to it."

"Where's Freda?"

"At the school, answering a ton of government questionnaires. She says she can do them better there than at home."

Hamish went back to the police station to find Jimmy waiting outside for him.

"Whisky, Hamish, quick."

"Come ben. You're lucky I've still got

some. How's it going?"

"It's not going anywhere. You were right. No drugs in either of them. No finger-prints on that cocaine packet. Does look like a setup."

"What about the postman?"

"The main post office said no deliveries were scheduled for Lochdubh after the usual nine-in-the-morning post. Whoever rode that bike wore gloves. But there is one thing: Strathclyde police found out that Jock has two addictions — whores and gambling."

"I wish I could go down to Glasgow," said Hamish.

"Why?"

"To find out more about Jock's back-ground."

"Man, Strathclyde police have been into it, and they wouldn't welcome you on their turf. Are you going to pour that whisky or not?"

"Sorry. I haven't had a day off since this all started. What's to stop me taking a wee trip in a private capacity?"

"I'd never get it past Daviot."

"He wouldnae need to know."

"All right. But just the one day."

"Where's Robin?"

"She's being transferred to Inverness

next week. And the latest is she's been pulled off duties as well until she goes. Haven't seen that woman reporter friend of yours. Hey, no romance there, is there? You're not really going because of her?"

"No, I never did fancy her," lied Hamish.

"Mackenzie's called 'Auld Iron Knickers' at headquarters. There's a lot there tried to get a leg over but didn't get anywhere."

"Is that a fact?"

"I'll let you go to Glasgow, but make sure Daviot doesn't hear of it."

Hamish drove down to Inverness the next day and caught the Glasgow plane. Two women in front of him irritated him by twisting around and trying to get a look at him. Both had newspapers, and both were giggling.

At Glasgow airport, he stopped at a kiosk to buy a copy of the *Bugle* to see if maybe Elspeth had anything to add to what he had found out. On the bus into the city, he flicked through the newspaper and then stared in horror at a feature by Elspeth called "The Don Juan Policeman of Lochdubh." It was a humorous little article claiming that one Hamish Macbeth had broken more hearts than any in the Highlands, and the latest heart to be broken was that of Detective Robin Mackenzie, who'd had an affair with the local hero, only to be tossed aside.

When he got off the bus, he went straight to the offices of the *Bugle* and demanded to see the editor. He waited almost a quarter of an hour until he was shown upstairs and into the editor's office, where the editor, flanked by several other men, was waiting.

"I've heard a lot about you," said the editor, holding out his hand. "I'm Mark Liddesdale."

Hamish ignored his hand. "This article in your paper is slander and lies. I'm going to sue."

"What exactly is wrong with it?" asked Liddesdale. "Do sit down."

"No, I'd rather stand. It specifically claims I had an affair with a female detective. This is a pack of lies."

"Our lawyers checked with our reporter, Elspeth Grant. She says that Robin Mackenzie told her so herself."

"Get her in here!" raged Hamish.

The editor nodded, and one of the men left the room.

Elspeth was ushered in after a few minutes. She saw Hamish and gave a defiant little toss of her head.

"You say in your article, Elspeth," said Hamish, "that I had an affair with Robin."

"She told me!"

"Have you your notes?" demanded Liddesdale. "What exactly did she say?"

"I have them here. Let me see. She said, 'I'm sick of the police. You know, I always thought policemen would be honourable, but they're just rats like any other men. Take you to bed one night and claim the moral high ground the next. Makes me sick.' "

"And where in your notes does it mention Mr. Macbeth here?"

Elspeth flushed. "It doesn't. But, I mean, who else was she working with?"

"Robin Mackenzie is based at Strathbane police headquarters, which is full of men," said Hamish. "You jumped to the wrong conclusion, slandered me. I'm going to sue."

"Leave us, Elspeth," said the editor heavily. "I'll deal with you later." After she had left, Liddesdale said, "Please do sit down. There is no need to drag this through the courts. We will print a full apology."

"I want it prominent, mind," said Hamish. "No burying it at the bottom of the sports page. And now to compensation?"

The editor rang a buzzer on his desk, and when his secretary entered, he said, "Take Mr. Macbeth here to the executive dining room and serve him coffee or drinks. We'll get back to you shortly, Mr. Macbeth."

Hamish left the newspaper office an hour later with a cheque for twenty-five thousand pounds in his pocket. He felt elated. What would his mother say when he gave her the money? The whole family could have a splendid holiday.

He heard his name being called and turned and saw Elspeth running up to him. "I'm sorry, Hamish. I thought —"

"You should have asked me, Elspeth. I thought a good reporter always checked the facts."

"If it's any consolation, I've been fired," said Elspeth.

"I'm right sorry, Elspeth. It was a grievous thing to do. Now leave me alone."

"Wait, Hamish. There's danger coming to you out of the loch."

Hamish made a sound of disgust and walked rapidly away. He knew that Elspeth often had uncanny psychic experiences, but right at that moment, he wanted to get as far away from her as possible.

CHAPTER ELEVEN

Truth is never pure, and rarely simple.
— Oscar Wilde

Hamish had asked Jimmy for Jock's address before he left. The artist lived in a flat off the Great Western Road.

Hamish started by interviewing the neighbours. An elderly couple who lived above Jock said they found him a nice, cheery sort of man. No, no wild parties or anything like that. The people below said much the same thing. But an artist, Hugh Tarrington, lived in the basement and turned out to know Jock very well.

"Can you paint here?" asked Hamish, looking around the dark basement.

"This is a garden flat," said Hugh. "I've built a studio out back."

Hugh was a thin, pale, bespectacled young man who looked more like an office worker than an artist. He fussed about, making tea, talking the whole time.

"I often go for a drink with Jock. He's great company," said Hugh. "He also used to spend a lot of time down here to get away from the wife. He said she was accusing him night and day of having an affair."

"And was he?"

"Truth to tell, I think there were a lot of women in Jock's life. Here's your tea. Mind you, I could swear he was actually in love."

"When was this?"

"Just before the divorce."

"Did he talk about it?"

"No, but he was obviously dying to. He talked a lot about love generally. His eyes were all shiny and his face soft."

"When did you first notice the signs?"

"Let me think. Oh, I know. It was that time after he came back from Brighton."

"Brighton!" exclaimed Hamish. "Are you sure?"

"Sure as sure. He brought me a box of fudge with 'A present from Brighton' on the lid."

"Do you know where I might find some folk who knew Jock well?"

"You could try his favourite pub, the Red Hackle in Byres Road. I'll come with you."

They walked together along to the pub. The Red Hackle turned out to be that rare thing — a pub that had escaped gentrification. It was dark and smoky with a long bar, a few tables, an old pinball machine, and a snooker table.

They ordered drinks. "There's Jerry. He knows Jock," said Hugh. He called Jerry over and introduced Hamish.

Jerry was a huge, shambling man with hands like hams and shaggy grey hair. "A policeman from the Highlands," he exclaimed. "I've been reading about the murders up there. What's Jock got himself into?"

"Nothing, I hope," said Hamish quickly. "But can you both tell me if he was into drugs?"

"Not Jock," said Jerry. "Wouldn't touch the stuff. Said he had enough trouble with the booze."

"Did he talk about his trip to Brighton?" asked Hamish.

"That was a time ago. He said he'd had the time of his life. I asked if he'd cleaned up. He's a gambler. He said he'd fallen in love. There was a crowd of us in that night, and we all started teasing him and asking for the name of the lady. He clammed up tight and said he had been joking, and we couldn't get anything more out of him."

I'd like to get into his flat, thought

Hamish, even though the police have already searched it.

He asked more questions but could not get any relevant information. He left Hugh in the pub and made his way to Jock's flat. He went quietly up the stairs. Outside the flat door, he took out a little bunch of skeleton keys and got to work on the lock until it sprang open.

It was a spacious Victorian flat with high ceilings. In the living room, there was a long bench filled with paints and brushes. The air smelled strongly of turpentine. There was a battered roll-top desk against one wall. He sat down in a chair in front of it, pulled on gloves, and began to go through any papers he could find. There were the usual bank statements and gas and electricity bills. The trouble was, thought Hamish, in these days of texting and e-mails, people did not often send personal letters through the post.

He pulled out drawer after drawer. And then in the bottom one, he found an envelope with a Brighton postmark.

He gently opened it and slid out the letter from inside.

He heard a slight noise behind him and made to swing round, but he was too late.

A heavy blow struck him on the back of

his head, and he tumbled off the chair on to the floor, fighting with the blackness that was trying to engulf him, hearing soft footsteps moving rapidly away.

When he could sit up, he felt terribly sick. He heaved himself to his feet, made his way groggily to the bathroom, and was violently ill. He splashed his face with cold water and gingerly felt his head. There was a large lump. He couldn't call the police because he wasn't supposed to be in the flat — or in Glasgow, for that matter.

When he went back to the desk, it was to find that the letter with the Brighton postmark was gone.

He went out of the flat, carefully locking the door behind him. He caught a taxi in the Great Western Road and asked to be taken to the nearest hospital. It was only in books, reflected Hamish, that the brave detective soldiered on. He knew he'd better get checked out.

He waited in the outpatients' until a doctor was free to examine him. He was told that, yes, as he knew, he had suffered a slight concussion, but the skin wasn't broken. "Been in a fight?" asked the doctor.

"No. Slipped in the bathroom and banged my head on the bath," lied Hamish.

"You'll need to take it easy," said the doctor. "We'll just take a few X-rays and send the results on to your own doctor."

Hamish knew that the mills of the National Health Service ground exceedingly slowly and that the results would end up on Dr. Brodie's desk in about a month's time.

He still felt sick when he left the hospital, and the light hurt his eyes. He peered at his watch. Just time to catch the plane. If only he could think clearly. Someone knew he was in Glasgow, and that someone must have been following him.

On the bus to the airport, despite the heat of the day, he felt cold and began to shiver. I'll go straight to bed when I get home, he promised himself.

He was queuing up at the gate for the Inverness plane when a voice behind him said, "It's never Hamish Macbeth!"

Hamish turned round. "Harry Wilson?" he asked.

"The same."

"I haven't seen you in ages," said Hamish. "Where are you off to?"

"Back home to Lairg for a break."

"What are you doing now?"

"Same as you, in a way. I'm a police diver."

"I thought you were going to be a football star."

"Played for Rangers for a bit but really wasn't up to the mark. Took the police exams. I got interested in diving after I joined the Glasgow Diving Club."

They had their tickets checked, then walked together to board the plane. "Are you all right?" asked Harry. "You're as white as a sheet."

"I was investigating something. You're not to tell anyone, mind. I wasn't supposed to be in Glasgow as far as the police were concerned. Someone crept up on me and bashed me on the head."

"You'd better go to your doctor when you get back to Lochdubh. What happened exactly?"

As they sat together on the plane, Hamish told him about breaking into Jock's flat.

"Someone must have been following you," said Harry. "Who knew you were going to Glasgow?"

"Only my boss, Jimmy Anderson."

"I thought that one would have died of liver failure by now, and what do you mean your boss? Isn't that old scunner Blair still in charge?"

"He's out of commission. Took a tumble

down some steps and broke his arm and his collarbone."

"Couldn't happen to a nicer fellow."

They parted at Inverness airport, Harry promising to visit Hamish in Lochdubh before he went back to Glasgow.

Hamish drove carefully homewards. The light hurt his eyes even more, and he put on sunglasses.

At the police station, he found the cat and dog were out. He had phoned Angela before he had left and had asked her to open the door for them at certain times during the day.

He still felt ill, so he went out again and walked to Dr. Brodie's. Angela opened the door to him, her thin face sharpening in concern. "You look dreadful, Hamish."

"Someone hit me on the head. I had it looked at in Glasgow, but I'd feel better if your man could take a look as well."

"I'll get him. Sit down, Hamish."

Hamish sat down wearily at the kitchen table. Three of Angela's cats leapt on the table among the dirty dishes and laptop and stared at him with unblinking eyes.

Dr. Brodie bustled in. "I'll take you to the surgery, Hamish, and examine you."

In the surgery, he gently examined

Hamish's head. "How did this happen?"

"Someone crept up behind me in Glasgow and socked me on the head."

"There's a big lump, but the skin isn't broken."

"The hospital in Glasgow is sending on the X-rays."

"Good. I'll need to keep a close eye on you, Hamish. You may experience dizziness, headaches, and weakness in the legs. I'm surprised the hospital didn't keep you in for observation."

"I had to get away. I wasn't supposed to be in Glasgow, and I didn't want the police to know I had been detecting on their patch."

"Go home and get some sleep. Phone headquarters and tell them you are taking time off. Come back tomorrow, and I'll have another look at you."

Hamish left the surgery to find Lugs and Sonsie waiting for him on the road outside.

"Come on home," he said. "I'm going to get something to eat and go to bed."

At the police station, he phoned Jimmy and told him about the letter with the Brighton postmark and then about being knocked down.

"I'll get straight up to see that sister, Caro. She may have known Jock before."

"I should go with you."

"You'd better rest. At least take tomorrow off. I'll see you in the morning and let you know how I get on."

Hamish fed the dog and cat. Then he heated up a can of soup for himself but only ate half of it. To his horror, tears began to run down his cheeks and he started shivering again.

He heated up two hot-water bottles and put them in his bed. He took a hot shower and then, followed by his pets, climbed wearily into bed. His last waking thought was that there should be some woman around to look after him.

Caro opened the door to Jimmy Anderson and a policewoman. "What now?" she asked in alarm.

"I think we'd better go inside," said Jimmy.

The policewoman sat in a chair in the corner of the room and took out her notebook.

"Now, Miss Garrard," began Jimmy, "you knew Jock Fleming before, didn't you?"

"Of course not."

"We have proof that you knew him in Brighton," lied Jimmy.

Her eyes dilated with fright, and then she said, "I didn't want to say anything about it. It would look so suspicious."

"Let's have the real story."

"I have a gallery in Brighton where I sell my stuff. He came in one day, and we got talking. Effie wasn't there. She was already up here. I had two postcards from her pinned up behind my desk. They were scenic views of Lochdubh. He said it looked like a beautiful place and where was it? I told him Lochdubh in Sutherland. He took me out for a drink."

"You had an affair with him," said Jimmy flatly.

She hung her head. "It was a one-night stand. He left Brighton the next day."

"And have you seen him since you have been up here?"

"I phoned him at the hotel. He shouted at me. He said he wished he'd never set eyes on my sister. He told me to leave him alone. He said he'd kill me if I told the police about our fling because they suspected him already and he didn't want them knowing anything else."

"I should charge you with withholding information," said Jimmy heavily. "Is there anything else you haven't been telling us?"

"No."

"And there's no way Effie could have known you had an affair with Jock?"

"No. I wanted to tell her, but I couldn't."

"Why not?"

"Effie was always jealous of me. I felt it would only make her obsession worse if I told her. She would go mad trying to prove to me that she had succeeded where I had failed."

"I want you to stay in Lochdubh and hold yourself ready for further questioning. PC Ettrick here will type up your statement. Report to the police unit in the morning and sign it."

Betty Barnard was walking along the waterfront in the morning when she saw Dr. Brodie leaving the police station. She stopped him. "Is Hamish ill?"

"He's had a bit of a concussion, but I think he'll be all right if he takes things easy."

Betty let herself into the police station. She walked into the bedroom. "How did you get concussed, Hamish?"

"I slipped and struck my head on the bath."

"I tell you what, that bed looks uncomfortable. Get up and sit in a chair in your living room, and I'll clean the sheets for you. Do you have a washing machine?"

"It's in a cupboard in the living room. It's one o' the kind you wheel up to the kitchen sink and put a hose on the tap, but don't bother. I'm fine. You shouldnae be here."

"Nonsense. You look dreadful. Up you get."

As Betty washed the sheets, she thought that the machine ought to be in a museum. The day was dry and sunny with a fresh breeze. She carried the sheets out into the back where there was a washing line and pinned them out to dry.

When she came back in to where Hamish was huddled in an armchair, she asked, "Where's your clean linen?"

"In a cupboard in the bedroom."

Betty put clean sheets and pillowslips on the bed and then helped Hamish back into it. "Now, what about breakfast?"

"I couldn't eat anything, Betty. I think I'd like to go to sleep again. Thanks a lot."

She dropped a kiss on his forehead. "You go to sleep, and I'll see you later."

Hamish fell back into a deep sleep and awoke six hours later. He felt much better and ravenously hungry. When he went into the kitchen, he noticed Betty had cleaned up everything and laid the table with two fresh baps — those Scottish bread rolls that everyone always claims are never what they used to be — on a plate along with a pat of butter, a pot of jam, and a thermos of coffee.

He ate the baps and then fried himself a plate of bacon and eggs. Hamish found himself getting very angry indeed at whoever it was who had struck him.

He had just finished eating when Jimmy appeared.

"Is it all right to talk to you?" asked Jimmy anxiously. "I would have called earlier, but Dr. Brodie called in at the unit and said no one was to disturb you."

"I'm better now. How did you get on with Caro?"

Jimmy told him. "If I were Blair," he said, "I would arrest Jock. But we haven't any hard evidence. I think that ex-wife of his and Jock did the murders. I think they're both twisted and sick. God, I'd like to break them."

"Where are they now?"

"Back here. They got lawyers. Nothing really to hold them on. Oh, I saw that Priscilla of yours."

"She isn't mine. What did she want?"

"She's off back to London."

"Did you tell her I was ill?"

"Yes, she sends her best wishes."

Cold, chilly bitch, thought Hamish with a sudden burst of fury. Didn't even bother to call to see if there was anything she could do for me. His fury was then replaced with a burst of gratitude for Betty's kindness.

I'm tired of being single, he thought. I am damn well going to ask Betty to marry me.

"You know," Jimmy was saying, interrupting Hamish's thoughts, "I think if it wasn't Jock or his wife, it could be Caro. She's got a history of mental illness. She was furious with her sister for having pinched her work. She may have fallen in love with Jock herself. She covered up that she'd met him before. Then Hal told his ex that he was going to marry."

"It's an idea," said Hamish slowly. "I mean, Hal must really have been a very lonely man. Nobody liked him. He'd be easy prey. Someone wanted that notebook of his."

After Jimmy had left, Hamish brought in his clean sheets, folded them, and put them in the cupboard. Then he dragged an old deck chair into the front garden and settled down with piles of notes he had made on the case.

The murders had been thought out, of that he was sure. But the murderer had been extremely lucky in that no one had seen him — or her. Jock Fleming seemed capable of arousing strong passions. Hamish began to wonder why Jock's marriage had really broken up. Apart from his general womanising, Jock liked whores. Hamish was willing to bet that Jock knew Dora was a prostitute before he married her. So why had they divorced?

"Coo-ee!" Hamish looked up from his notes. Gloria Addenfest was standing on the other side of the hedge. "The funeral's tomorrow," she said. "Mr. Wellington's been great. You going to be there? Eleven o'clock."

"Wouldn't miss it," said Hamish.

"See ya." She waggled her fingers at him and walked off.

If there was something Lochdubh liked more than a wedding, it was a funeral, especially when it was the funeral of someone they had not cared about one bit. When Hamish walked along to the church the next morning, black-clad figures were heading towards the church from every direction.

The church bell tolled out across the loch. Outside the church, the band of the Argyll and Sutherland Highlanders stood, getting their instruments ready, fighting for space with the television crews.

The church was full to capacity. Hamish found a pew at the back where he could observe the congregation.

In the front pew sat Gloria Addenfest in full Hollywood mourning: black cartwheel hat with thick black veil; black tailored suit.

The organist began to play "Abide with Me," and everyone shuffled to their feet as the coffin was carried in. Hymns were sung, a dignified sermon was delivered, there were readings from the Old and New Testaments, and then the small coffin was hoisted up and everyone fell in behind it for the procession up the hill to the graveyard, led by the pipe band playing a dirge.

Mr. Wellington read the words of the burial service. A lone piper played "Amazing Grace" — what else? thought Hamish. I bet Gloria chose that — as the coffin was slowly lowered into the grave.

Then the whole band struck up "Scotland the Brave," and with pipes skirling and kilts swinging, they led the "mourners" down the hill to the church hall.

The hall was lined with buffet tables with every sort of Scottish delicacy from smoked salmon to grouse in aspic to sherry trifle. A bar at the end was covered in whisky bottles and glasses. Someone had obviously advised Gloria not to waste her money on fine wines. There were tea urns and coffee urns.

At first, everyone talked in low murmurs, discreetly piling plates with food and taking them off to one of the tables that had been set up around the hall.

Gloria accosted Hamish. "I'm glad you came," she said. She had removed her hat.

"Did anyone warn you this is likely to go on all night?" asked Hamish.

"Why?"

"It's a highland funeral. In some of the outer isles, it can still go on all week."

"They all seem subdued."

"Give them time."

After an hour, the whisky began to flow and the voices got louder. After another two hours, the floor was cleared and the local band of accordion, drums, and fiddle started playing highland reels.

Hamish had drunk nothing but water, but his head began to ache. There was no sign of Betty, Jock, Dora, or Caro. Poor Effie, thought Hamish. No grand send-off for her. Effie had been cremated quietly and quickly in Strathbane.

He went back to the police station and took two aspirin. He was suddenly exhausted again and felt like crying. If only life were like television, he thought crossly, where the hero is tied up and beaten to a pulp, escapes his captors, and manages to still engage in a brutal fistfight. He sighed. Bruce Willis I am not.

He took his notes to bed with him, searching, always searching, for a clue he felt sure was in there. He fell into a deep sleep, the notes scattered about him in the bed.

He dreamt that Elspeth was calling him from the other side of the loch. He knew he had to reach her. He waded into the loch and found it was shallow. He continued wading towards her on the other side, and then his foot slipped and he plunged down into the depths of the loch. He tried to rise to the surface, but something caught him by the ankle and held him down.

He awoke with a start. Elspeth. She had

done an awful thing to him and had been punished. But he suddenly wished it had never happened. He remembered the cheque from the newspaper. He had forgotten all about it. He got out of bed and searched in the pockets of the trousers he had worn to Glasgow. The cheque was still there. He laid it out on the bedside table to remind him to put it in the bank in the morning.

He thought again about Betty. What did she really think of him? It would be pleasant to be married to someone easy and kind.

Why had Priscilla gone off so coldly, particularly when she knew he was ill?

Hamish rose early in the morning and went for a walk along the waterfront. He liked rising early in the summer to enjoy the light. The winters were so long and dark and one hardly ever saw the sun.

The loch was like a mirror. He went along to the harbour where the fishing boats were coming back in. They were now allowed to fish only three days a week. The fishermen were furious because they said European countries did not have to obey such stringent laws. Lochdubh had been a fishing village since the days of the Highland Clearances in the early nineteenth century. Crofters driven off by landowners who wanted the land for sheep were sometimes forced over to the coast, where they were told they could make a living from seaweed gathering and fish. Lochdubh had been luckier than most other places because the Countess of Sutherland had built a summer home there — now a deserted hotel by the harbour. She arranged for a whole village to be built out of rows of stone whitewashed houses, the houses that still stood there today.

Hamish hailed Archie Macleod. "Good catch?"

"Fair to middling. I'll give ye a wee fish for Sonsie. I'll drop it by the kitchen door."

"Thanks, Archie."

"Lucky we got anything. So many seals around."

Hamish knew that no fisherman in Lochdubh would ever contemplate killing a seal because they believed that seals were human beings who had come back.

He sat down on the harbour wall, warm from the sun. Seals. One of the boys had said something about a seal.

He stiffened. What if Hal had been standing looking up at the waterfront, waiting for someone, but that someone had

268

crept up out of the loch?

He stood up and looked along the water-front, and then he saw Betty.

He had only seen her wearing trouser suits before, but she was now wearing a pair of shorts. Her legs were very long and surprisingly thin. Must be why she always wears trousers, thought Hamish.

She was standing on a flat stone by the water's edge, her hands behind her back, peering down into the water.

Hamish was suddenly reminded of the heron he had seen with Robin. There was something predatory in Betty's stance, and those long thin legs reminded him of the heron's legs.

For some reason he could not explain to himself at the time, he moved quickly back from the harbour wall so that she would not see him.

He went back to the police station to look for Harry Wilson's number. He found he was very cold again and put it down to the after-effects of the concussion.

CHAPTER TWELVE

*From the mountains, moors, and
  fenlands,
Where the heron, the Shuh-shuh-gah,
Feeds among the reeds and rushes.*
     — Henry Wadsworth Longfellow

"Harry," said Hamish, "can I come over and see you? I need your help with something."

"Tell you what, Hamish. I feel like a bit of a drive. I'll nip over and see you. Give me about half an hour or so."

"Have you got any photos of your diving school, that one you went to?"

"I've got some in the family photo album. I'll bring the lot."

After Hamish had rung off, Dr. Brodie came by. He shone lights in Hamish's eyes and checked the lump on his head. "I think you'll do," he said. "How are you feeling otherwise? Not too emotional?"

"I cry a bit."

"That happens. Any weakness in the legs?"

"No, they're all right."

"Headaches?"

"I had one at the funeral celebrations."

"You weren't drinking too much?"

"Wasn't drinking at all."

"Good, because Lochdubh is one great hangover, and I'm plagued with the usual: 'But, Doctor, I only had two drinks. It must be something I ate.' Take care of yourself. I saw your boss, Mr. Daviot, and told him firmly you needed peace and quiet."

When he left, Hamish waited impatiently for Harry's arrival. Harry had said he would arrive in half an hour or so, which by the highland clock could mean as much as two hours. As they say in the Highlands, "mañana" is too urgent a word.

An hour and a half later, Harry arrived. "Sorry, Hamish," he said. "Sheep on the road."

Sheep on the road was another of those highland lies, like "I've just had two drinks," "I've a bad back," and "I'll fix it for you right away."

"I've got the coffee on," said Hamish. "Did you bring the photos?"

"Yes, but why do you want to see them?"

"It's this idea I have that the murderer of

the American could have come out of the loch. Jock Fleming, the artist, is from Glasgow. So is his wife. Maybe one of them took a diving course at one time."

"Here you are." Harry fished a large photo album out of a duffel bag and put it on the table.

"The ones of the diving school are at the back."

Hamish opened the leather-bound album to the back. There were a lot of photos of scuba divers going into the sea and coming up out of the sea. But he found one of a Christmas party. He eagerly studied the faces, but there was not one single one he recognised.

"Is this all you've got?"

"Pretty much," said Harry.

Hamish sat back in his chair, disappointed. Then he said, "Was it mostly men?"

"Yes, pretty much. We got the occasional woman, but usually they didn't stay the course."

"Remember anyone who did?"

"There was one woman, Sarah Jerome. Middle-aged and quite plump, but she turned out to be a natural. Then a tall thin woman — what was her name? Harriet something or other. She was pretty good."

Hamish sat sunk in thought. Then he said, "Of course, it's a long shot thinking it might have been someone who was there at the same time as you. Could you go into the office and use the phone? Call the diving school and ask one of the instructors if there was any woman who passed the course with flying colours. Then ask if Jock Fleming or Dora Fleming was ever a member."

"Right. Where's the office?"

"Just through to the right, next to the bedroom."

Harry seemed to be on the phone for a long time. At last, he came back.

"The name Betty Barnard mean anything to you?"

Hamish put his head in his hands.

"Are you all right?" asked Harry anxiously. "Not having a dizzy spell? Want me to call a doctor?"

Hamish took his hands away from his face. "No, I'm all right now. Tell me about Betty Barnard."

"She took the course last year. The instructor said he had never seen anyone learn so quickly. Said she was a natural. Someone you know?"

"Oh, yes. May be nothing to do with the murders. I'm not being very hospitable,

Harry. But I've got to get going on this case."

"That's all right. I've got a friend over at Cnothan I want to see."

After he had left, Hamish thought wearily: If she did it, why? The rooms at the hotel had been thoroughly searched. He didn't remember any report of diving gear.

He suddenly thought of Elspeth. He felt that by his rudeness, he had somehow driven her into writing that silly article. Now she was out of a job. He went into the office and dialled her home number. When she answered, he said, "It's me, Hamish. Don't hang up. Elspeth, I may just have found out who the murderer is. If you get up here fast, maybe I'll have a story for you that'll get your job back."

"Thanks, Hamish," she said. "I'm so awfully sorry."

"Just get up here. You can stay in the cell here."

"I'll be there by this evening."

Hamish drove up to the Tommel Castle Hotel. He sat for a moment in the car park, looking at the hotel and remembering simpler days when it was a private residence.

Then he got out of the Land Rover, entered the hotel, and went into Mr. Johnson's office.

274

"Hullo, Hamish," said the manager. "Help yourself to coffee. I wish you'd solve these murders. Bookings are a bit thin on the ground."

Hamish poured himself a mug of black coffee and sat down wearily. "Tell me, Mr. Johnson, if someone wanted to hide a diving outfit — you know, diving suit and tanks and all that — is there anywhere in this hotel they could hide the stuff?"

"Let me see. It'd need to be someplace the maids don't clean. They're good girls and not lazy, so there are few places. There's the storage room in the basement, but if someone wanted to leave anything there, they'd need to ask me for the key. We had a couple here last year who skipped out without paying. They'd run up a huge bill. They left their suitcases behind, and I put them in that storage room. I thought they'd turn out to be full of rocks, but there was some expensive clothes in there. I keep meaning to sort them out and give them to charity."

"I'd like a look at the place."

"I'll give you the key. Just walk down the back stairs and you'll find it."

He opened the safe, saying over his shoulder, "I keep all the spare keys here. We used to have them up on a board, but in these evil days, we decided it was a bit too risky. Here you are." He extracted a large key and gave it to Hamish.

Hamish thanked him and made his way down the back stairs. In the old days, he thought, the servants' quarters would all be down here. He was wishing he'd asked Mr. Johnson which one was the door of the storage room. There were so many doors. He tried them one after another until he came to one that was locked.

He unlocked the door and swung it open. Maybe Betty had just taken the diving gear up to the moors and sunk the lot in a peat bog. But diving equipment was expensive. Yet how would she get the key to this storage room if it was locked in the safe?

There was a window letting in pale light, set high up on the wall. He edged his way through broken furniture, suitcases, and old steamer trunks until he was under the window. There was a steamer trunk under it. He climbed up on it. He put on gloves and pushed the window upwards. It opened. And it opened enough, he noticed, to let someone climb in and drop down into the room.

He turned and looked around. If he found anything, he needed witnesses. He took out his mobile and called Jimmy and spoke rapidly.

Hamish waited until he heard footsteps on the stairs coming down. Jimmy came in, followed by two detectives and a policeman.

"What have you got for us, Hamish?"

"I haven't searched yet. I need witnesses in case I find anything." He told Jimmy his theory about the diver and how Betty Barnard had taken a course in scuba diving.

Jimmy sighed. "Sounds like a complete flight o' fancy to me, Hamish. But now we're here, we may as well get on with it." He turned round and said, "We're looking for a diving suit and diving gear. It means opening up any cases or boxes. Get to it."

Hamish went back to the window and looked round the room. She wouldn't have carried the gear openly. Maybe she put it in a big strong garbage bag. If she met anyone, she could say she was looking for somewhere to dump extra rubbish. She would slide down from the window after throwing the stuff down first. She would pull the steamer trunk under the window so that she could climb out again.

He studied the dusty floor and then the pile of trunks nearest him. He took out a magnifying glass and began to study the trunks. He saw faint marks in the dust. He moved the top trunks until he got to a large leather-bound one at the bottom.

He lifted the lid. I really didn't want to know, he thought sadly. Lying in the trunk was a rubber diving suit, with goggles and tanks.

"Here, Jimmy," he said.

Jimmy came hurrying over. "I'd better get the forensic boys in here. Should be enough DNA on that mask."

Hamish gingerly lifted an edge of the diving suit. "Leave it!" ordered Jimmy.

"Look at this," said Hamish.

Under the suit was a notebook Hamish recognised. "That's Hal's notebook," he said.

"Right. We'd better take her in for questioning. Good work, Hamish. How on earth did you think of it?"

"It was the heron," said Hamish sadly.

"Are you sure you're all right? You're rambling."

"Never mind."

"Want to come up and make the arrest? It's your collar."

"No, that's fine. I'm feeling a bit shaky. I'll chust get back to the police station."

Hamish sat down at the table in his kitchen and stared into space. How could he have been so stupid?

He remembered the laughter and the sunny days. He remembered how Betty had looked after him when even Priscilla had cleared off and left him alone. He had even been thinking of marrying her. There had been no sign of wickedness in her. I think it's the first time I've been well and truly fooled, he thought miserably, and all because I was starting to dream of getting married. Maybe we're all dreamers and fantasists, like poor Effie.

The phone in the office rang shrill and loud. He went to answer it. It was Jimmy, his voice sharp with anger.

"She's gone!"

"Whit?"

"Gone. And it's all the fault of that gabby porter and even gabbier manager. Sammy, the porter, asks Johnson what the police are doing now. Johnson says Hamish Macbeth is down in the storage room looking for diving gear. 'That should help with his poaching,' said Sammy, who considers himself no end of a wit. So when Betty Barnard walks into the hotel, he decided to try the joke out on her. Result: she's gone. Left everything behind and scarpered. We've got roadblocks set up, and police are watching all the ports,

279

railway stations, and airports."

"I'm going to see Dora Fleming," said Hamish. "I think that one knew more than she was telling us."

"Okay. Get back to me."

Hamish went out and walked along to Sea View. He turned in the doorway and saw that the cat and dog had followed him. "Stay there," he ordered.

"What now?" asked Mrs. Dunne.

"I want to see Mrs. Fleming."

"I telt her to pack her bags and get out. I won't have drugs in this house."

"Where did she go?"

"I don't know. But I tell you this: No one in Lochdubh would have her. That artist came and helped her with her bags."

Hamish ran back for the Land Rover, the dog and cat loping behind him. He put them in the police station and drove up to the Tommel Castle Hotel.

"Is Jock Fleming in?" he asked Mr. Johnson.

"No, he wanted his ex-wife to move in, but enough's enough. I only gave him a free room because he was painting Priscilla's portrait. I told him to find other accommodation."

"Do you know where they went?"

"They wanted cheap accommodation, so

I told them to try the caravan park over at Cnothan. Hamish, I'm right sorry about Sammy . . ."

But Hamish was already out the door.

The caravan park was situated outside Cnothan. Hamish went to the office and asked if a Mr. and Mrs. Fleming had booked a caravan, and he was directed to one over against the wall near the entrance.

He knocked at the door. Jock opened it and scowled. "What now?"

"Let me in," said Hamish. "You've been withholding valuable information."

Jock stood aside. Hamish removed his cap and walked past him. Dora was sitting at a table at the far end.

"Betty Barnard," said Hamish, "killed Hal Addenfest, and so she killed Effie as well. I do not believe you pair divorced because Jock discovered that you, Dora, had been a prostitute. I think you found out that Jock had been having an affair with Betty. Maybe after the divorce, Jock, you went off Betty, but she was still in love with you. The hold she had on you was that she sold your paintings like no one else could sell them. But she was crazy about you. Crazy enough to kill, and I think you suspected it all along. You may as well tell me, because when she's caught, it'll all come out. She's made a run for it. Where would she go?"

Jock hung his head. "I can't think. Maybe Glasgow."

"Betty wouldn't go back there when she knows the police are looking for her."

"Honestly I can't think of anywhere else."

"When that cocaine was found in Dora's room, didn't you suspect Betty?"

"I didn't. Honest. I thought there was some madman on the loose."

"You should have told me about Betty. It might just have stopped that American from being murdered. I'll get back to you, Jock. Not only me but Jimmy Anderson will have a lot of questions to ask you."

After Hamish had left them, he phoned Jimmy and told him where they were.

"Still not a sign of the Barnard woman," said Jimmy. "That bleeding artist can get his paints out and draw us a picture of her."

"No need," said Hamish heavily, "I have a photo of her."

"How did you get that?"

"We were friendly. We went out on a picnic once, and I took my camera. The film hasn't been developed, but I'm heading back to Lochdubh. I'll meet you at the police station and give it to you."

"Everyone's on to digital cameras these days," grumbled Jimmy. "This camera of yours should be put in a museum."

"Don't complain. There's the film."

"Why did we never think of Betty Barnard?"

"Because she seemed the only sane one of the lot of them," said Hamish. "I thought the hotel was searched from top to bottom."

"Not really their fault. They were concentrating on the rooms, not the basement. I'll get off to Strathbane with this film. If I hurry, we can just make the morning edition of the newspapers with her photo."

After he had gone, Hamish decided to visit Caro. He felt she had a right to know that her sister's killer had been found.

Caro eyed him warily when she opened the door to him. "What now?"

"Can I come in? We've found who killed Effie."

She looked at him with startled eyes and then turned away as he followed her in.

"Who is it?" she asked.

"Betty Barnard."

"What? But she was up here the other

day. She was going to be my agent, and I was very excited because she is so high-powered. How? Why?"

"The how is because she turned out to be a champion diver. She came out of the loch to attack the American. She killed him, so it stands to reason she killed Effie. I can only guess she was crazily in love with Jock. When Effie said she was pregnant, Betty must have been so mad with jealousy that she believed her."

"What did she say when you arrested her?"

"We haven't got her. She's on the run. But don't worry. We'll catch her."

Caro sat down and looked up at the tall figure of the policeman. "So," she said slowly, "she must have been as obsessed as poor Effie."

"Though in her case, a fantasy turned into reality," said Hamish. "Most people just dream of killing someone. She put it into action. What is it about Jock Fleming that drives women mad? He just seemed at first like a nice, easy-going fellow."

"He exudes a strong sexual excitement and danger. I think some people carry around a sort of strong chemical in their make-up. I was drawn to him myself."

"Will you go back south now?"

"I don't know. Brighton is so noisy and crowded. It is so beautiful here."

"Don't leave Brighton yet," said Hamish. "The winters here can be awful, long, and dark."

"Do you get much snow?"

"Occasionally we get terrible blizzards, but we're near the Gulf Stream, and that keeps us a bit milder than central Scotland. But it's a lonely life up here on the moors."

"I'm only a short drive from the village. If I stay, the first thing I'll do is get that corrugated iron off the roof and replaced with tiles. When it rains, the noise just goes on and on."

When Hamish got back to the police station, it was to find Elspeth had arrived. Although he had locked up the station, Elspeth, like the locals, knew he kept a spare key in the gutter above the door.

"Right, Elspeth," he said. "Get out your notebook, and I'll tell you what I know." Hamish experienced a sudden guilty pang. He had promised Matthew the story.

Elspeth wrote busily. Hamish broke off to say, "Remember, you got this information from the hotel staff. You can say we're hunting for Betty Barnard, because her photo's going out to the papers tonight. Chust say she's wanted for questioning."

"Why did she do it?"

"I don't know if you can say this. Well, maybe you can say it's local speculation that she was in love with Jock Fleming. It was well known in the village that Hal took notes. He may have seen something relating to the murder and told Betty. I think she romanced him when nobody was looking and then phoned him that night and arranged to meet him on the beach. She probably drove down to the far side of the loch and got into her diving gear in the shelter of the trees, dived into the loch, and swam across. He was so intent on staring up at the waterfront, waiting for her to arrive, that he didnae hear her coming."

"I'll say it's thanks to your brilliant deduction that they found out it was her," said Elspeth.

"No, give Jimmy Anderson the credit. He's been marvellous to work for."

"If you say so."

"Go into the office. You can use my computer, type it out, and e-mail it across. I'll make up the bed in the cell. I'd give you my bed, but" — he hesitated and then went on defiantly — "the dog and cat aye sleep wi' me."

"The cell is fine, Hamish."

When Elspeth went off into the office, Hamish took the dog and cat out for a walk and then returned to get dinner ready. Archie had left six mackerel on the kitchen table. Hamish cooked one for Sonsie and then fried some liver for Lugs. He boiled potatoes, and when they were nearly ready, he took two of the mackerel, gutted them, dipped them in egg, rolled them in oatmeal, and fried them in the pan.

He then put a bowl of oatmeal on the table and a block of butter.

When Elspeth came back in, he asked, "All done?"

"Yes, finished and sent over."

"Sit down and help yourself."

Elspeth speared a fluffy potato, rolled it in the oatmeal, and ate it with a lump of butter before tackling the fish.

At the end of the meal, the phone in the office rang. Hamish went to answer it.

"Liddesdale here," said the voice at the other end. "Remember me? I'm the editor of the *Bugle*."

"Yes?"

"Elspeth Grant has filed a great story, but we're nervous about using it before checking with you first."

"Read it to me," said Hamish.

He listened as Liddesdale read it over. When he finished, Hamish said, "My, I don't know where she got all that information from, but it's accurate. She always was the best."

"You sound as if you've forgiven her."

"We go back a long way. Look, if you give her her job back, I won't cash that cheque."

"You're kidding!"

"No, I mean it. I havenae cashed it yet."

"That's very generous of you. But it's already gone through the books. Just keep it. Do you know where Elspeth is?"

"She checked a lot of the facts with me. Strathbane will be sending you a photo of Betty Barnard. Elspeth's around and about. She's got her mobile phone with her. If you don't want her, she'll probably get herself a job on the *Daily Record.*"

"She doesn't want to go to them," said Liddesdale. The *Daily Record* was their biggest rival. "I'll speak to her."

Hamish went back into the kitchen. "That was Liddesdale checking your story. I told him you were thinking of applying for a job on the *Record.* He's going to phone you on your mobile."

Elspeth's phone in her bag rang.

She took it out and went back through to the office. She was on the phone quite a long time. Then she came back.

"I've got my job back. Hamish, Liddesdale says you even offered to give them their money back if he re-employed me."

"Chust a thought," mumbled Hamish, rattling the dishes in the sink.

"After all I did to you, too. I don't know how to thank you."

"Let's talk about something else, Elspeth. You'll need to do a follow-up."

"I'll get up first thing in the morning and interview everyone at the hotel."

"I've still to make up the bed for you."

"I'll come and help you."

In the cell, Hamish said, "The bed's awfy hard. I'll put a quilt under you, if you like."

"No, I'm so tired and relieved, I'll fall straight asleep. Where are your beasties?"

"Gone to bed." He straightened up. "Well, that's that. I'll give you first use of the bathroom."

Elspeth looked up at him and suddenly clutched his arm. Her grey eyes had turned silver. "What is it?" asked Hamish.

"Something bad, something evil. Quite near."

"You're tired, Elspeth. We all get fancies when we're tired. Let's go back to the kitchen and have a dram. I hope Jimmy's left me some."

They sat back at the kitchen table with glasses of whisky.

"Look at the cat!" said Elspeth.

Sonsie was standing at the entrance to the kitchen, fur straight on end, eyes blazing.

"What's up with the beast?" said Hamish. He half rose from the table just as the kitchen door crashed open and Betty Barnard stood there, a gun in her hand, her eyes glittering with anger.

She had dyed her hair blonde and cut it short and was wearing a pair of dark glasses, but Hamish knew it was Betty.

"You bastard," she spat at Hamish. "I'm taking you with me."

"Where?"

"The grave."

She levelled the pistol and took aim.

With one fluid motion, the cat sprang straight at her face. The cat was heavy, and the force of the spring knocked Betty backwards. Lugs came running in and sank his teeth into her leg. Hamish stamped on Betty's wrist and bent down and grabbed the gun.

"Off, Sonsie," said Hamish.

"Get it away from me!" screamed Betty. Sonsie was crouched on Betty's chest, staring into her eyes. The cat drew back her lips in a long hiss.

Hamish bent down and moved the cat. He twisted Betty round and, grabbing a pair of handcuffs from the dresser, handcuffed her hands behind her back.

She was now babbling with fear. "Keep the cat away from me. Keep it away!"

Hamish took off his belt and bound her ankles. He went through to the office and phoned Strathbane.

When he came back, he hoisted Betty upright and placed her on a chair. Elspeth left the room, muttering, "Got to phone."

Hamish looked at Betty sadly. "Why?"

"Mind your own business," she snarled, and refused to say another word.

It was half an hour before Hamish heard the welcome sound of sirens in the distance. The wait had felt like days.

Elspeth had come back into the kitchen. She stood in a corner, staring at Betty.

Just as Hamish heard the police cars draw up outside, the phone in the office rang. He went through and answered it. It was Liddesdale. "Mr. Macbeth, Elspeth has filed an extraordinary story about Betty Barnard trying to kill you."

"It's all true," snapped Hamish. "Print the damn thing."

He went back just as Jimmy came into the kitchen.

"She was going to kill us," said Hamish. "That's the gun on the table."

Jimmy charged Betty and told the police to take her to Strathbane. "You two had better come along as well," said Jimmy. "I'll need your statements. I'd think you'd want to be in on the questioning, Hamish."

At Strathbane, Jimmy sat in an interview room, flanked by Daviot himself. Hamish sat quietly in one corner. Once the interview tape was put into the machine, Jimmy began the questioning.

"We have you for the murder of Hal Addenfest and the attempted murder of PC Hamish Macbeth and Miss Elspeth Grant, so you may as well start by telling us why you killed Effie Garrard."

There was a long silence. Then she said harshly, "May I smoke?"

Jimmy nodded and slid a packet of cigarettes and lighter over to her. She lit one, blew smoke, and leaned back. "Funny," she said, "I gave these cancer sticks up years ago. Oh, why not?

"Jock and I had an affair. He said he loved me, and at that time, he was telling the truth. Then he began to cool. I told him unless he divorced Dora, I wouldn't represent him any more. Furthermore, I had lent him money for his gambling debts, and I said I would demand repayment. So he divorced Dora, but he kept making excuses. But the affair continued." Her voice suddenly trembled. "I was so terribly in love with him.

"Then I heard that Effie Garrard had flipped and was saying that Jock was going to marry her. I went to see her. I told her he wanted nothing to do with her. She told me he loved her and he'd had an affair with her. I knew Jock had passing affairs, but it was when she said she was pregnant that I believed her. I knew she was a bit long in the tooth to get pregnant, but these days women have babies even in their fifties. I'd an awful feeling it might be true and Jock might feel obliged to marry her.

"I had a spare bottle of antifreeze in my car. I went into the hotel bar. It was empty that evening. I asked the barman to help me see if I had dropped my car keys in the car park. When he started to go towards the door, I took a bottle of sweet wine from the bar and put it behind a chair. Then I ran after him and said I'd found the keys. I went back to the bar with him and ordered a martini. While he was busy mixing it, I got the bottle, took off my jacket, and covered the bottle with it. I drank that martini in one gulp.

"I ran into Jock on the road out. He said he'd spoken to Effie and told her he was off to Geordie's Cleft in the morning. I asked him where it was, and he told me. I said did Effie know where it was? He said sheepishly that he'd told her and no doubt she'd be climbing up the mountain in the morning to haunt him.

"I wrote a note supposed to come from Jock saying he loved her and asking her to bring the wine up to Geordie's Cleft at midnight and they'd celebrate their engagement. 'You can start without me,' I wrote. 'I've already had a swig of it.' I opened the wine and poured most of it out and then poured in the antifreeze and screwed the cork back in. I left the bottle and note outside her door. Then on the road back to the hotel, I threw the antifreeze into the River Anstey.

"I climbed up to Geordie's Cleft the next night. I almost hoped to find she wasn't there, but she was dead and wearing that engagement ring. I took out my pen-knife and sawed it off and threw the ring in the heather on my way back. I put the suicide note in her pocket. I felt nothing. I felt I had really had nothing to do with it. Then that American came up to me with his notebook. 'I have it all here,' he said. 'I was looking in the window of the bar, and I saw you steal that bottle of wine. I think the police would be very interested.'

"I asked him what he wanted. He amazed me by saying he wanted to get married, that he was tired of living alone. He said he was lonely and he couldn't understand why nobody liked him.

"I said I'd meet him on the beach the following night at midnight and let him know my decision. I never thought he'd fall for it, but he did. Maybe because I said I was lonely, too, and that I'd like him to be a bit more romantic and the beach at midnight would be romantic.

"I flew down to Glasgow and got my diving gear, came back up, and hid it in the boot of my car. I drove over to the forest on the far side of the loch. I dived in and swam underwater across the loch.

"I saw him standing there like a bloody garden gnome staring up at the road. I crept up, picking up a rock as I went, and hammered him on the head. He fell backwards. I took the notebook. I dragged him by the ankles. I was going to take him with me into the loch. There's a sort of shelf down there, and I was going to lodge the body under it. Then I heard those two schoolboys. So I left him, waded in, and dived. I knew the police would be searching the rooms, and I thought of filling my diving suit with stones and sinking it down into the loch, but it was expensive gear. I knew about the storeroom because the porter had told me about the people who hadn't paid their bill and how their luggage was down there. I searched around the outside of the hotel with a torch until I found the right window. I shone the torch on that notebook and went through it. There was nothing about me stealing the wine."

Hamish's quiet voice interrupted her. "Why was I hit on the head in Glasgow? How did you know I was there? What was so important about that letter from Brighton?"

"I was always wary of you," she said. "I followed you when you left for Glasgow. I had to hang well behind before you got on to the busier roads. I saw you take the Glasgow plane. It was crowded. I bought myself a hat and dark glasses at the shop at the airport, bought a ticket, and took a chance. You never even noticed me. I followed you while you talked to people. Then I followed you back to Jock's flat. I was worried what you would find. I stood inside the door and watched you take that letter from Brighton out. Jock and I went to Brighton for a weekend once. I stayed behind. I wrote him a passionate love letter. Jock kept a baseball bat by the door. I whacked you with that and took the letter, went to the airport, and got the next plane back to Inverness."

"When Jock was in Brighton, he managed to have a one-night stand with Caro Garrard. How did he manage that?"

"He couldn't have . . . He wouldn't."

"Okay, maybe he met her and went back to Brighton later. But did you know Jock was still having sex with his wife?"

"Liar. Not possible. He told me he was sick of her and she'd only followed him up here to get more money out of him."

"We have forensic proof that he did," said Hamish. "He said something about her having certain tricks."

Her eyes grew wider and wider, and then she began to scream and scream.

"Take her away," said Jimmy. "That's enough for now."

After she had gone, Hamish said, "Just as well she didn't know, or we'd have another dead body."

"Have you and your lady friend made your statements?" asked Daviot.

"She is not my lady friend, but yes, we have made our statements."

"I think the least we can do," said Daviot, "is to put you and Miss Grant up in a hotel for the night."

"Thank you, sir, but we should be getting back. Her luggage is there, and I have to look after my animals. The cat saved my life."

"The medical officer treated that bite your dog gave her," said Jimmy. "Okay, off you go. You're looking very white again, Hamish. Sure you're up to driving back?"

"I'll be okay."

Hamish and Elspeth drove back in silence for most of the way. Then Hamish said, "I plan to do absolutely nothing tomorrow. You?"

"I'll do a follow-up piece in the morning. You know the stuff — the shadow of murder leaves Lochdubh and yackety-yak."

"At least with the attempt on our lives, I've got a good excuse for not giving Matthew the story. I promised him first bite. I think we should go out to the Italian's tomorrow and celebrate the end of all this."

"You're on." Elspeth grinned in the darkness. "And for once in your life, you've got the money to pay for it."

Although he was exhausted, Hamish did not fall asleep right away. He now knew that Betty had been nice to him only to throw him off the scent. Had he become such a pathetic bachelor that he could not see what lay behind her attractive appearance?

Sonsie stretched out beside him and gave a rumbling purr. He patted the cat's silky coat and slowly drifted off into tortured dreams in which Betty was dragging him down into the black depths of the lake.

Hamish awoke late the next morning to find Elspeth had gone out. He washed and shaved and decided not to put on his uniform but to take the day off. He had just finished dressing when the phone rang. It was Jimmy.

"Betty Barnard is asking to see you, Hamish. You don't need to."

"I'll drop over. Is she still at police headquarters?"

"Until this afternoon. We're transferring her to the women's prison to await trial."

Hamish drove off, taking Sonsie and Lugs with him. He could let them out for a run in the heather on the road back.

The day was grey and misty. As the Land Rover mounted a rise above Strathbane, he looked down on the place he loathed most. He always thought the town a scar on the beauty of the Highlands.

He parked outside police headquarters and went up to the detectives' room where Jimmy was waiting. "I'll take you down to the cells," said Jimmy. "Daviot is thrilled to bits. He's about to hold a press conference."

"I hope you took all the credit," said Hamish uneasily.

"You're still frightened of promotion in case they take you out of that backwater called Lochdubh. Relax. I did a Blair. I took all the credit."

Hamish was led to Betty's cell. The door was left open, and a policewoman stood on duty outside.

Betty was sitting on the cell's narrow bed. She looked up when he came in.

"I just wanted to say goodbye," she said.

"Why?" Hamish sat down on the bed next to her.

"We were friends, believe it or not. I even began to think at one time that it

300

might be nice to be married to someone like you."

"Why did you have to go and murder two people and ruin your life?" asked Hamish.

"Passion," she said. "Have you ever really been in love, Hamish? Deep, all-consuming love? It tricks the mind. Jock always had some excuse. 'We'll get married next year, or when I've had the next exhibition,' and I believed him because love had driven me mad.

"I've asked my lawyer to contact Jock and tell him to come and see me. Even now I can't let go."

There were voices outside, and then the policewoman came in and handed Betty a letter. She opened it up and glanced at the signature. "It's from Jock," she said.

She read the letter while her face grew stiff with pain. Then she numbly handed it to Hamish. Jock had written:

Dear Betty,

I am not coming to see you and I will never forgive you for what you've done. I never really wanted to marry you but you'd lent me money I couldn't pay back and you were such a good agent I thought I'd string you along. Don't contact me again.

Jock

Hamish sat in an awkward silence. Then he said, "Well, that's that. You'll chust need to get on with life."

"In prison?"

"Why not? No death penalty. It didn't come out at the interview, but it was you that defaced the portrait of Priscilla, wasn't it?"

"I got sick of him raving on about her beauty. Oh, God, help me! I don't know what to do."

Hamish stood up. "There's nothing you can do but take your punishment. Have you no remorse for killing these two people?"

"No. I despised them both."

Hamish left the cell, and the policewoman slammed and locked the cell door behind him.

EPILOGUE

Never give all the heart, for love
Will hardly seem worth thinking of
To passionate women if it seem
Certain, and they never dream
That it fades out from kiss to kiss.
— W. B. Yeats

As he drove back down into Lochdubh, Hamish saw the mobile unit being towed away.

He found he was looking forward to his evening with Elspeth.

She was in the bathroom when he entered the police station. "Is that you, Hamish?" she called nervously.

"Only me. Betty's locked up tight. Don't use all the hot water."

"I already have. You'd better stoke up the fire."

Hamish lifted the lid of the stove and added kindling and peat to the dying fire.

It was grand to have Elspeth for company, he thought. They'd been through a

303

lot together. Her psychic abilities were better than the seer's any day. He felt like going up to Angus and demanding his fish back.

The phone rang. What now? He went into the office. Jimmy's voice sounded down the line, harsh and upset.

"She's hanged herself, Hamish."

"What? How?"

"With her tights on the bars of her cell."

"I thought they would take anything like that away from her."

"There's going to be an enquiry, and that means statements and forms and bureaucracy by the mile. You'd better come over tomorrow and make a statement about her condition when you saw her last."

"I'll send it over, Jimmy. I'm heartsick about the whole business."

"Well, it'll save the state a trial."

"Did she leave a note?"

"She wrote on the back of a letter from Jock Fleming. It simply said, 'You've killed me, Jock.'"

Hamish felt a sudden burst of anger. "I'm going over to see that bastard tomorrow. If he hadn't been stringing her along, these murders might never have taken place."

"Don't punch him," said Jimmy wearily, "or he'll charge you with assault and you'll lose your job."

"I'll keep my hands behind my back."

"Good man."

"How's Blair?"

"Who cares? As far as I know, he's back home convalescing. See you."

Elspeth came out of the bathroom. She was made-up and wearing a filmy gown of green silk chiffon and high heels.

"You look a picture," said Hamish. He bent and kissed her cheek. "I'll put on my best suit."

"You mean your only suit," said Elspeth.

He went off into the bathroom to shower and then into the bedroom to dress.

Elspeth smiled to herself as she heard him whistling. Everything was going to be all right.

The phone rang. Hamish went into the office.

"Hamish?" said Priscilla's voice.

"Who else?" said Hamish coldly.

"Hamish, I saw the story in the newspapers, and I think I should explain."

"Explain what?"

"I was on my way to see you when I met Betty Barnard. She asked me where I was going, and I said I was going to see you because Angela Brodie had phoned me to say you had a concussion. Betty said, 'Don't worry. As his future wife, I think I should be the one to take care of him.' I now realise she was probably lying."

"Why did you believe her?"

"I had seen the pair of you together. I thought you were in love with her, Hamish."

Hamish gripped the receiver hard. "Tell me, Priscilla, if at the time you believed Betty, why should you care? You're engaged to be married."

"*Was* engaged to be married."

Hamish could feel his heart beating hard. "Was?"

"Yes. I broke it off as soon as I got back. It wasn't working out. I'm tired of London. I'm thinking of coming back and working at the hotel. I miss my home."

"That'll be grand. When?"

"I'll need to give a month's notice. After that, I suppose."

"I'll look forward to it."

Hamish said goodbye and slowly replaced the receiver. She was coming home for good. Priscilla was coming back. But she hadn't said why she was so upset when Betty lied to her about marrying him.

He finished dressing and went into the

kitchen. Elspeth smiled at him and said, "Don't you look . . ." and then the smile faded from her face.

"Priscilla," she said flatly. "That was Priscilla on the phone."

"Yes."

"And?"

Hamish's face flamed. "It wass a private conversation."

"You poor sucker. She keeps jerking your chain."

"You've got no right to speak to me like that."

Elspeth sighed. "One's as bad as the other. She sat at this table one evening and told me how she was looking forward to her wedding to dear Peter."

"I don't want to talk about her!" howled Hamish.

"You may as well take me for dinner," said Elspeth. "Otherwise I'd be all dressed up and nowhere to go."

Hamish and Elspeth tried to make conversation during dinner, but their silences lengthened.

"This is hopeless," said Elspeth finally. "Stay and finish your wine. I'm going back to pack."

"Stay the night."

307

"I'd rather stop somewhere on the road. Thanks for the story, thanks for getting me my job back, and I hope you and Priscilla Halburton-Smythe will be truly miserable."

She stalked out.

Hamish stayed where he was, feeling guilty. But as he saw her car drive past, a surge of elation went through him. Priscilla was coming home to the Highlands.

The next day, Hamish drove over to the caravan park at Cnothan.

Jock and Dora were sitting on deck chairs outside their caravan.

"Betty's dead," said Hamish, standing over them.

"How? What happened?" asked Jock.

"She got your letter and hanged herself in her cell. You are a piece of scum. If you hadn't led her on, she might never have murdered those two folk."

"Och, get off your high horse. Don't tell me you've never led some woman on."

A picture of Elspeth rose before Hamish's eyes. He shook his head to get rid of it.

"Don't cross my path again," he said. "In fact, get off my beat, or I'll make your lives a misery."

Hamish stalked off. Then he had a sudden thought. He got into the Land Rover and telephoned Jimmy. "Betty didn't say anything about sewing the cocaine into the curtains when I was there."

"We interviewed her later when she stopped screaming. We had to fill in the blanks. Yes, she confessed to that and to defacing Priscilla's portrait."

"Pity," said Hamish. "I'd ha' loved to arrest one of that pair."

As Hamish drove back towards Lochdubh, he suddenly thought of Detective Chief Inspector Blair. He felt sure no one had gone to visit him. He wrestled with his conscience and then decided a ten-minute call would be all right.

He bought a bottle of whisky and drove to the housing estate in Strathbane where Blair lived.

It was a semi-detached house with a weedy garden in front. He rang the doorbell and waited, hearing shuffling from inside.

Blair opened the door and blinked up at Hamish. He was leaning on a pair of crutches.

"What is it?" he demanded.

"I brought you a present and came to see how you were," said Hamish.

Blair snatched the bottle from him, snarled, "I know you, you came to gloat. Bastard!" and slammed the door in Hamish's face.

Hamish walked away, shaking his head and giving his conscience a talking-to. "Now, wasn't that a waste of time?" he raged. A woman passing by gave him a nervous look.

He drove into the centre of Strathbane and parked the Land Rover. He would take a look around the shops and treat himself to lunch.

Hamish was not used to having money to spend on himself, and he felt quite profligate as he bought himself a new pair of shoes, his old ones having fallen apart a long time ago. The odd times he had worn a suit, he had worn his regulation boots with it.

He was just leaving the shoe shop when he saw Robin Mackenzie on the other side of the street. Hamish hailed her. "I thought you were in Inverness."

"I came up to get the last of my stuff. I was just taking a last look round," said Robin.

"What about lunch?"

"All right. There's quite a good Chinese here."

Inside the restaurant, Hamish asked her, "How do you think you'll get on in Inverness?"

"It's not too bad. Better than Strathbane. I know I did the wrong thing, Hamish, but so did Daviot, and the way he got on his moral high horse makes me sick."

"Aye, but the man's at that dangerous middle age, and when a young woman like you throws herself at him, he's easy prey."

"Never mind. Tell me all about the case."

Hamish talked as they ate. When he finished, Robin asked, "So what happened to Effie's mobile phone?"

"I don't know. You should still have been on the case. Went right out of my head."

"All you need to do is get the number and ring it. The battery might still be working."

"I may do. But what's the point? Betty will never go to trial now."

"Why?"

"She hanged herself with her tights in her cell."

"Saves a trial."

They finished their meal. Robin said, "If you're ever down in Inverness, give me a call." She took a card out of her handbag.

"That's my new number."

"Thanks. I will."

Hamish stopped off at the Tommel Castle Hotel on the road back.

"I'm right sorry, Hamish," said Mr. Johnson. "How was I to guess that a woman like Betty Barnard was a murderess?"

"It's over now. How's business?"

"Not very good. Cancellations coming in every day."

"Let me think."

Hamish slumped down in an armchair on the other side of the manager's desk and closed his eyes. He was silent so long that Mr. Johnson finally asked, "Have you fallen asleep, Hamish?"

Hamish opened his eyes. "This is a fake castle, right? Built in Victorian times, but it looks spooky. You need a ghost. People love ghosts."

"Now, how do we get a ghost?"

"We need someone who was killed here in the nineteenth century or someone who committed suicide. You tell the staff the plan. They won't want to be laid off because of lack of customers, so they'll play along. I'll see Matthew Campbell when you're ready and start the ball rolling.

Then what about murder weekends?"

"Hamish, what are you talking about?"

"Some hotels have murder weekends. You get a sort of Agatha Christie script. Everyone dresses up in twenties or thirties clothes and takes a part. They've all got to guess who the murderer is."

"Could be an idea."

"Get on the Internet and find out where they do it and what they charge."

"I don't know if Colonel Halburton-Smythe will agree to the idea."

"He may not, but Priscilla will. She's coming back to live here." Hamish's hazel eyes glowed.

And you'll get hurt all over again, thought the manager. Aloud, he said, "That's good. She's a grand worker. What are you going to do now? Take a holiday?"

Hamish opened his mouth to say he was going to New York and closed it again. Priscilla was coming home, and he wanted to be in Lochdubh when she arrived. But that's not for a month, said a voice in his head. Plenty of time to go to New York.

I can't leave my animals, he thought, relieved to find a genuine excuse. No one in the village would look after Sonsie.

"Hamish, your lips are moving, but no sound is coming out."

313

Hamish blushed. "Sorry, I was thinking. I'll take some time off just to potter around and relax."

Back at the police station, there was an urgent message from the minister, Mr. Wellington, asking Hamish to call at the manse.

He went round to the kitchen door at the back, knowing the front door was hardly ever used.

Mr. Wellington let him in. "I have a problem of conscience," began the minister.

"I'm surprised you can't cope with it yourself."

"Sit down."

Hamish sat at the kitchen table. The manse kitchen was a large gloomy room dating from the days when there would be at least six servants living in at the manse.

"It's like this," said Mr. Wellington. "Jock Fleming called on me. He wants me to remarry him to his ex-wife. I do not wish to do it."

"Why?"

"Because his presence in this village brought murder with it. I feel it should have been my Christian duty to marry him, and yet I could not. I asked him if he believed in God and Jesus Christ, and he laughed and said, 'No more than you do. I'm like the rest of Scotland. Church is for births, marriages, and deaths.' "

"You did the right thing. I want the man out of here as well. Tell you what. I'll go and see them and speed them on their way."

Hamish drove to Cnothan, taking his pets with him. At the caravan park, he was told that Mrs. Fleming had left but that Mr. Fleming was staying on.

Hamish drove into the village of Cnothan. He braked to a halt when he saw Jock. The artist was talking to one of the local girls, Fiona Crumley. As Hamish watched, Jock bent forward and whispered something in Fiona's ear, and she blushed and giggled.

He got out of the Land Rover. "A word with you, Jock."

"See you later," said Fiona.

Hamish watched her go and then said, "I want you out of here, Jock. I warned you."

"I like it here. You can't force me to go."

"Shouldn't you be back with Dora? I hear you wanted to marry her."

"Och, that was just to keep her quiet. I got rid of her by telling her to go to Glasgow and find a minister."

"Why the church? Why not a registry office?"

"Dora wants a white wedding."

"I'm warning you for the last time. Get the hell off my beat."

Jock laughed and walked away. Hamish set off down the main street in pursuit of Fiona. He caught up with her at the loch side — that grim black loch man-made by the Hydro Electric Board.

"A word of warning for you," said Hamish. She looked at him round-eyed. "Keep clear of Jock Fleming. I think you should know he's got syphilis. Oh, he'll swear he hasn't, but I'd hate to see a lassie like you catching a nasty sexual disease."

"Thanks, Hamish. He seemed so nice."

"And warn your friends."

The news of Jock's fictional syphilis spread like fire in the heather out from Cnothan and across to Lochdubh. Hamish was lucky that no one actually confronted Jock with the fact that he had the disease. They simply shunned him. He was told his caravan was needed for a pre-booking and no other van was available. Shops refused to serve him. Hamish was relieved when he finally got the news that Jock had left.

Hamish thought several times about

phoning Elspeth but each time couldn't muster up the courage. After all, what could he say? He had no right to string her along. But wasn't he as bad as Effie, getting excited about Priscilla coming back? Wasn't he a fantasist as well?

His spirits were dampened somewhat by an unexpected visit from Colonel Halburton-Smythe. The fussy little colonel walked into the kitchen one morning when Hamish was washing up dirty dishes. He sat down at the table unasked and looked around him.

"To think my daughter might have been living here," he said.

Hamish stacked the last clean dish on the rack and leaned against the counter. He wondered if all retired military men who insisted on being addressed by their army rank were as infuriating and pompous as Priscilla's father.

"Did you come to criticise my home?" he asked.

"I came about this idea you put up to Johnson. It's mad."

"What's mad about it?"

"Ghosts and murder. Haven't we had enough real murder in Lochdubh already without manufacturing fictional ones?"

"So don't do it. Lose customers. What do I care?"

"Don't be so hasty. Tell me about it."

So Hamish patiently described his ideas. The colonel studied him after he had finished with shrewd little eyes. "Wouldn't such an idea bring in the riff-raff?"

"Not if you charge enough. Tell me, at country house parties, don't they still dress up and play charades?"

"Yes."

"Well, there you are. People love dressing up. If you ferret around in the trunks in the storage room, you'll probably find enough thirties and twenties clothes to save you buying any."

"I'll think about it."

"What about the ghost? Any murdered people in the castle's past?"

"In the early part of the twentieth century, the then Lord Derwent killed his wife. A maid witnessed him throwing her down the stairs. It never went to court, and the maid was paid off."

"There you are. The ghost of Lady Derwent haunts the castle, crying for justice."

"So I need to pay someone to play the ghost and keep their mouths shut?"

"No, then they'd all know it wasn't real. I know someone who could fix up ghostly effects for you."

"I'll think about it. Horrible business

318

about that artist having syphilis, and to think he was painting my daughter! I'll be off."

"Aren't you going to thank me for my great ideas?"

"Oh, they are a bit ridiculous. But thank you for trying." He marched out.

Later that day, Hamish did not know whether to be amused or furious when Mr. Johnson said that the colonel had gathered the staff together to tell them about "his" great ideas about a ghost and murder weekends.

That evening, Gloria Addenfest called on Hamish. "Came to say thanks," she said. "I'm off to the States. I'm glad it's all over. Funny. I liked that Barnard woman. I thought she was the only one around that was any fun. All goes to show what a great judge of character I am. I even asked her to visit me in New York."

"She fooled us all," said Hamish heavily.

"Here's my card anyway. You can come and stay with me any time."

After she had left, a voice nagged in his head that he should go. Priscilla would be as distant as ever. But what would he do with his cat?

His next caller was Jimmy Anderson.

"Tell me, Jimmy," said Hamish, opening a bottle of whisky and putting it in front of the detective, "did Betty say anything at the subsequent interview about what she did with Effie's mobile phone?"

"Didn't ask her. Doesn't matter now. What's this rumour going around that Jock has syphilis?"

"I put it about to get rid of him. His wife had left, and he was already chatting up some young girl in Cnothan. I hope that's the last we ever see of him. He'll always bring trouble."

"I hear you went to visit Blair," Jimmy said.

"How did you find out?"

"He phoned up drunk and weepy and said nobody had bothered to find out how he was except Hamish Macbeth."

"The old scunner. I took him a bottle of whisky. He grabbed it from me and slammed the door in my face. It's a wonder that man isn't dead."

"I think God keeps him on this earth to remind us that suffering purifies the soul."

Hamish poured himself a small measure of whisky. "I saw Robin in Strathbane."

"How's Auld Iron Knickers getting on?"

"Fine. She likes Inverness."

"Someone said, mind you, and if you

can believe this, that they had seen Robin down in Inverness arm in arm with Daviot."

Hamish manufactured a laugh. "Now, that really is daft. Daviot, of all people."

"That's what I said. So are you going to take your holiday now?"

"Starting as soon as possible. Like now."

"So where are you going?"

"Och, I'm chust staying here," said Hamish awkwardly.

"You know, every time I drive into peasantville, I look to see what the hell it is that keeps you here, but I'm blessed if I can."

"Never mind. Make that your last whisky this evening. One of these days you're going to run off the road."

"All right, mother." Jimmy swallowed his whisky. "Here's hoping we never have to cope with another murder again."

Hamish was in Patel's shop the next morning when Angela came up to him. "Have you seen the *Bugle*?"

"No, why?"

"Jock's been shot. Elspeth's written the story."

Hamish bought a copy of the newspaper and went outside and sat on the waterfront wall.

Jock had been shot dead in his flat. Neighbours heard the shot. They found his flat door open and Jock lying dead on the floor. Police said that Jock Fleming owed considerable sums of money to loan sharks to pay for his gambling debts, and they felt that was the reason he was killed. Then there was an inside feature, also by Elspeth, about Jock's connection to the murders in Lochdubh. The article ended by saying that it was reported that prices of his paintings had doubled.

Hamish wondered for a moment whether Dora had decided she'd had enough of Jock's philandering but then came to the conclusion that probably one of his loan sharks had wiped him out.

He pottered about for the rest of the day, feeling the peace of Lochdubh beginning to seep into his bones. In early evening, just as the sun was setting, he decided to go for a walk along the beach.

The air was clear and slightly cool. Thin wisps of cloud trailed the sky above, heralding a change in the good weather.

And then as he looked along the beach, he saw a heron, standing on the flat rock where Betty had stood, looking down into the water.

As he approached, it slowly turned its

head and looked at him.

He experienced a sudden superstitious shiver of fear. He ran towards it, waving his arms and shouting, "Go away. Shoo!"

The bird lazily opened its great wings and sailed off down the loch in the direction of the Atlantic.

Hamish Macbeth watched it until it was out of sight.

In Brighton, businessman George Bentinck had just returned from working in South Africa. He was expected to attend a Rotary Club dinner, and he wanted a female companion to take along. His wife was dead, and he didn't want to sit at the table where all the other men would be flanked by their wives or companions.

He phoned various lady friends, but all said they were too busy. He looked through his address book again. Then he saw the name Effie Garrard. He remembered her as a plain little woman he had met at a gallery opening. She had insisted on him writing down her mobile phone number. He had been too busy in South Africa to read any newspapers and was blissfully unaware of murder in the north of Scotland.

He dialled.

Deep in the heather, protected from the elements, down below Geordie's Cleft, Effie's phone, which she had charged up on the night she met her death, began to ring.

Like a faint cry for help, it shrilled tinnily out into the soft clear highland light.

But there was no one to hear it.

Not even the ghost of a dreamer.

We hope you have enjoyed this Large Print book. Other Thorndike, Wheeler or Chivers Press Large Print books are available at your library or directly from the publishers.

For more information about current and upcoming titles, please call or write, without obligation, to:

Publisher
Thorndike Press
295 Kennedy Memorial Drive
Waterville, ME   04901
Tel. (800) 223-1244

Or visit our Web site at:
www.gale.com/thorndike
www.gale.com/wheeler

OR

Chivers Large Print
published by BBC Audiobooks Ltd
St James House, The Square
Lower Bristol Road
Bath BA2 3BH
England
Tel. +44(0) 800 136919
email: bbcaudiobooks@bbc.co.uk
www.bbcaudiobooks.co.uk

All our Large Print titles are designed for easy reading, and all our books are made to last.